He lifted his head to
tempt, taking in he
ance, the golden ha
shoulders, her lips
kisses.

'You want me to
you give yourself away by behaving like a whore!'

Giulia felt as if her heart had stopped beating. Helplessly she stammered, 'I—I don't understand . . .'

'Do you take me for a fool?' His eyes were almost black with anger. 'Oh, you look like Caterina—very like. 'Tis these that betray you . . .' Roughly he seized her hands and turned them over to stare at the work-reddened palms. 'As I suspected, you're the maid-servant!'

Elizabeth Hart was born in Kent and brought up and educated in Sussex. She worked as a secretary with the BBC for six years, then took a teacher training course and taught for fifteen years in England and Switzerland. She now lives on the Isle of Wight.

She gave up teaching five years ago to concentrate on writing both for children and adults. *A Wedding in Venice* is her second Masquerade Historical Romance.

A WEDDING IN VENICE

ELIZABETH HART

MILLS & BOON LIMITED
15–16 BROOK'S MEWS
LONDON W1A 1DR

All the characters in this book have no existence outside the imagination of the Author, and have no relation whatsoever to anyone bearing the same name or names. They are not even distantly inspired by any individual known or unknown to the Author, and all the incidents are pure invention.

The text of this publication or any part thereof may not be reproduced or transmitted in any form or by any means, electronic or mechanical, including photocopying, recording, storage in an information retrieval system, or otherwise, without the written permission of the publisher.

This book is sold subject to the condition that it shall not, by way of trade or otherwise, be lent, resold, hired out or otherwise circulated without the prior consent of the publisher in any form of binding or cover other than that in which it is published and without a similar condition including this condition being imposed on the subsequent purchaser.

*First published in Great Britain 1985
by Mills & Boon Limited*

© Elizabeth Hart 1985

*Australian copyright 1985
Philippine copyright 1985
This edition 1985*

ISBN 0 263 75001 9

*Set in 11 on 11 pt Linotron Times
04–0285–60,000*

*Photoset by Rowland Phototypesetting Ltd
Bury St Edmunds, Suffolk
Made and printed in Great Britain by
Cox & Wyman Ltd, Reading*

CHAPTER ONE

A YELLOW sun hung low over the plains of Lombardy as along the straight road lined with poplars came a travelling dust-cloud. Giulia, crossing the yard, shaded her eyes to watch until it resolved itself into two horsemen, then turned away with a shrug. Merchants from Venice, no doubt hoping to sell their latest spoils from the Turkish wars. Well, they would not make much profit here. Her master, Ercole Tebaldi, being a merchant himself, was known to drive a hard bargain.

She continued her way across the yard, hitching her kirtle above her knees. Her feet were bare, the weather being surprisingly mild for late October in this year of 1479, and she took care where she trod, for the hens were always finding new nesting-places. How she loved that moment of discovery, that first glimpse of brown shell half-hidden amidst the straw!

Already she had a clutch of speckled eggs held in her skirt when the horsemen arrived. They entered the yard at full gallop, scattering the livestock and almost running Giulia down before they wheeled to a halt, their horses lathered with sweat.

She turned on them angrily. 'Are you mad? Look, you've made me spill my eggs . . .'

Her voice tailed away as she took in their appearance, the like of which she had never seen before. Both were tall and bearded, but one was dressed outlandishly in a long tunic with a white silk turban on his head and a dagger at his waist, while the other, whom by his proud bearing she took to be the master, wore black hose and a black doublet slashed with red. His complexion was dark, though not so dark as his companion's, and this made all the more noticeable a pale scar curving like a scimitar across his high cheekbone. She thought him the handsomest man she had ever seen—and the most disturbing.

He swung himself out of the saddle and stood commandingly before her. 'I come in search of Ercole Tebaldi. The steward at his house in Verona told me I would find him here.'

The sharpness of his tone brought Giulia to her senses. 'This is indeed the country residence of Messer Tebaldi,' she said haughtily. 'What is your business with him?'

As if surprised by her manner he gave her a penetrating look, making her uncomfortably aware of her bare feet and dishevelled hair. 'My business with him is none of yours,' he snapped, his dark eyes glowering at her. 'Have the goodness to inform your master I am here.'

Giulia raised her chin. 'And how may I do that when you haven't even told me your name?'

'You're insolent, wench!' His fingers closed around her wrist, jerking her towards him. 'Were you *my* servant I would teach you better manners.'

'But happily, sir, I am not!' Her colour rising she tried to pull free from his grasp but his fingers only tightened, searing her skin.

He stared down into her flushed face, his eyes

narrowing. 'By the rood,' he murmured. 'Surely you cannot be Tebaldi's daughter?'

For a moment Giulia was amused that he should take her for Caterina. The very idea of Ercole Tebaldi's gently nurtured daughter gathering hens' eggs in the farmyard with her skirt hitched above her knees was quite incongruous! None the less it was not the first time such a confusion had arisen and could only mean this stranger must at some time have met Caterina—or at least have seen a portrait of her—to know of the resemblance between them. A small suspicion stirred in Giulia's mind.

'No,' she said guardedly. 'I am not Caterina.'

'For that at least I must be thankful!' He released her arm and stepped backwards to take up an arrogant stance, one hand resting lightly on the hilt of his sword. 'My name is Pietro Gabrieli. *Now* will you kindly inform your master I am here?'

So her suspicion was correct!

'I will go at once, my lord,' she murmured, and sped into the house.

She found her master at his desk, frowning over a page of accounts. A balding, once-handsome man, Ercole Tebaldi now wore a permanently anxious look on his good-natured face. Over the years he had allowed himself to become involved in increasingly risky ventures, driven by his wife's constant demands for fine clothes, more servants, a house in the country, and of course a substantial dowry for their only daughter Caterina. After all, as Monna Lucia never tired of reminding her husband, he had only to provide the money. It was she, with her aristocratic connections, who had succeeded in arranging an alliance between her daughter and one of the noblest families in Venice. Four years ago the thirteen-year-old Caterina had been formally betrothed to Pietro Gabrieli, a widower nearly twice her age—who had promptly left to command a State galley in the war against the Turks and had not been heard of since.

That is, until today . . .

Ercole stared incredulously at Giulia. 'You mean Pietro Gabrieli is here, in this house?'

'Yes, sir. At least, he's still outside in the yard at present. I thought I'd best come straight to warn you.'

'You did right, child.' He took out a handkerchief to wipe his perspiring face. 'I never thought to see him so soon . . . and yet I suppose 'tis only to be expected. Now that the war is at an end he has returned to put his house in order . . . and naturally the first thing he must do is claim his bride.'

'Had I not better inform Monna Lucia of his arrival?' Giulia interrupted, fearful that Pietro Gabrieli might be growing restive.

'What?' Ercole gave a start, betraying he had temporarily forgotten her existence. 'Oh, yes . . . inform my wife. No, wait—*I* shall inform my wife. You go at once to Caterina and bid her prepare herself to meet her betrothed.'

Giulia obeyed him, glad that she need not be the one to break the news to Monna Lucia, who would surely blame her for having left Pietro Gabrieli cooling his heels in the yard all this while.

She knocked on Caterina's door. A muffled voice called out, 'Who is it?'

'Only me . . . Giulia.' Without waiting for a command, she opened the door and stepped inside.

'Go away.' Caterina's voice, listless and tearful, came from behind the closed bed-curtains. 'I am unwell.'

'You must rouse yourself, madonna.' Giulia drew back the curtains, allowing daylight to stream in upon the girl lying in the bed. ' 'Tis past noon.'

Caterina groaned and turned her face into the pillow. 'I am ill, I tell you! Leave me alone.'

Giulia stared helplessly down at the slim, golden-haired girl who bore such an uncanny resemblance to herself. Theirs was a curious relationship, for they had virtually grown up together since Ercole Tebaldi brought the seven-year-old Giulia home from the foundling hospital in Venice to be a maid and companion to his daughter. Only a few months separated them in age; as they grew older and the likeness between them more apparent, inevitably there was gossip, but Giulia had learned to close her ears to it. She knew only that Ercole Tebaldi was a just master who showed her no particular favour above the other servants. As for Caterina, if she heard the gossip she gave no sign it troubled her, but continued to treat Giulia as a friend and confidante. Only in the last few months had there grown up a coolness between them—and Giulia knew all too well the reason why.

With a sigh she sat down on the edge of the bed, tucking one bare brown foot beneath her. 'You must try to forget Bernardo,' she said gently. 'You know very well your mother will never allow you to marry him.'

'But I *love* him!'

'I can't imagine why,' Giulia admitted frankly. 'He's such a solemn fellow.'

'He's gentle and kind.' Caterina gave a stifled sob. 'And he writes such beautiful poetry!'

Giulia sighed. Privately she considered Bernardo very dull. The son of a cabinet-maker, he had fallen in love with Caterina on seeing her every

Sunday at Mass, and eventually plucked up the courage to pass her a note. Giulia had become involved as a go-between, carrying messages between the lovers and trying to conceal their secret meetings from the sharp eyes of Caterina's mother.

Alas, she was not a good liar. Her brown eyes were too honest and revealing, and it had not taken Monna Lucia long to extract the truth from her. And then—what a commotion! How *could* Caterina have behaved in so wanton a manner, encouraging the advances of a penniless poet when she was already betrothed to a nobleman, albeit an absent one! Monna Lucia immediately swept her daughter off to the country, even though it was October and hardly a suitable time of year.

And for this Caterina blamed Giulia, who had betrayed her confidence. Hence the coolness between them.

Giulia wondered how best she could break the unwelcome news. At length she said casually, 'Of course, now that Venice has signed a treaty with the Turks and the fighting is over, 'tis only to be expected that Pietro Gabrieli will return . . .'

'I don't care if he does,' said Caterina. 'I shall refuse to marry him. And if they try to force me against my will I shall enter a nunnery!'

Giulia was alarmed by the intensity of Caterina's tone. She knew her young mistress was devout, even pious; none the less she could not imagine that Caterina would take kindly to a life of poverty and obedience, let alone chastity. She said reasonably, 'Would it not be best to wait till you've met him? He may turn out to be more agreeable than you think.'

'He's old!' snapped Caterina.

'Not more than thirty. And very handsome.'

'How do you know? You've never seen him.'

Giulia drew a deep breath. 'Oh yes, I have. He's downstairs at this moment, with your father.'

For a moment Caterina lay unmoving, as if she had not heard. Then she raised her head to stare disbelievingly at Giulia. 'Pietro Gabrieli . . . downstairs with my father?'

Giulia nodded. 'He went first to your house in Verona. The servants directed him here.'

Hectic colour flooded Caterina's cheeks, then drained away to leave them sheet-white. 'But what does he want?'

'To marry you, of course.'

'That's impossible!'

Giulia smiled. 'Wait till you see him. He's much better-looking than Bernardo. And he has with him a most remarkable servant.'

'I tell you, it's *impossible*!' Caterina burst into a storm of weeping, flinging herself back against the pillows.

As luck would have it, Monna Lucia chose this moment to enter the room. She was a thin, long-nosed woman with a discontented pucker to her lips, and on seeing her daughter's distress she rounded immediately on Giulia. 'Why is she upset? What have you been saying to her?'

Hastily Giulia stood up. 'Nothing, madonna. I only . . .'

'Look at you, girl! No shoes or stockings and your hair tumbled over your shoulders—What must Messer Gabrieli think of us, that we cannot afford a better class of servant?'

Giulia pressed her lips together, aware that it was useless to try to defend herself. Monna Lucia had always disliked her from the day she first set foot inside the Tebaldi household.

'And to leave him waiting outside while you told your master—Why did you not call me at once?' Without giving Giulia a chance to reply, Monna Lucia bent over her daughter, soothing back the hair from Caterina's damp forehead. 'There's no need to be afraid, my love. Pietro Gabrieli is as fine a man as you could wish . . . and most anxious to meet you at last. Come, you must put on your most becoming gown.' She turned back to Giulia, her eyes growing hard again. 'As for *you*, you can go down to the kitchens and make yourself useful for once. Extra hands will be needed to prepare a meal fit for our guest.'

Giulia fled at once, thankful to escape.

She found the kitchens abuzz with excitement over the unexpected arrival.

'Did you ever see such a proud-looking man?'

'Not too proud to seek a match with the Tebaldis! For all Monna Lucia boasts of her connections, the master's only a cloth-merchant, when all's said and done.'

'Aye, but a rich one! And the war has left the Venetians very low in their coffers. What better way for a man to replenish his purse than by finding himself a well-dowered bride?'

'Then the sooner he marries her the better, I say, or he may find the cabinet-maker's son has been there before him!'

The coarse laughter that greeted this sally brought a blush to Giulia's cheeks. Because of her strange situation in the household, betwixt and between, she never felt entirely at ease below stairs. As far as possible she tried not to be drawn into servants' gossip, even though this meant she was often accused of putting on airs.

'When will the wedding take place, then?'
'Ask Giulia. She's the one who's privy to the family's secrets.'
They turned to stare at her. Giulia tried to look unconcerned. 'Quite soon, I imagine. Messer Gabrieli seems rather impatient.'
Loud laughter, followed by more ribald remarks. Giulia was relieved when speculation was brought to an abrupt halt by the appearance of Pietro Gabrieli's servant.
He stood in the doorway, dwarfing everyone by his size, his huge hand hovering warily near his dagger. For a moment there was silence, then one of the pages pulled out a chair for him to sit on and another offered him a glass of wine. Silently he accepted the chair but waved away the wine.
After a while the conversation started up again, this time in whispers.
'An infidel slave, I tell you . . . probably captured in the siege.'
'Ssssh! There's a sharp edge to that dagger . . .'
'Don't worry. Most like he doesn't even speak our language.'
'Ask him his name. He must be able to tell us that, at least.'
They asked him his name. For answer he took a handful of flour the cook was using to prepare the fish, and spread it on the table. Then, with a blunt forefinger, he traced slowly and awkwardly the letters K—A—S—I—M.
'Kasim! Is that your name—Kasim?'
The servant nodded. Opening his mouth he pointed inside, making a strange guttural sound.
'He's had his tongue cut out! That's why he can't speak, poor fellow.'
Giulia shivered. How could Ercole Tebaldi even

contemplate sending a timid, gentle creature like Caterina to live in such a barbaric household?

'Hey, Giulia!' It was the cook who spoke. 'You'll be needed to wait at table tonight, with all these extra dishes. Best go put on your cleanest gown.'

The dining salon was a magnificent room, high-ceilinged and with doorways of sculptured marble. Torches already flared in their sconces, for the evenings had begun to draw in early, and in their dancing light the Tebaldi silver gleamed on the table. Sadly, it was only the second-best silver, to Monna Lucia's mortification, since they had not expected to entertain so important a guest while out of town.

Giulia, in her most presentable gown of dark grey wool, entered the room to place a flagon of wine beside her master. She could not resist stealing a quick glance at Caterina, who was clad in richly embroidered green silk with her blonde hair enclosed in a jewelled net. None of this finery, however, could disguise her sickly pallor or the glazed look in her eyes. Before her lay a plate of venison, untouched.

Instinctively Giulia's gaze travelled across the table to Pietro Gabrieli, curious to see how he was taking this far-from-flattering behaviour on the part of his betrothed. With a sense of shock she found his dark eyes fixed intently on her own face. He then looked at Caterina, a slight frown creasing his brow. Giulia could guess all too easily the thoughts going through his mind. She flushed and turned away.

'Our guest needs more wine.' Ercole's voice arrested her. 'Refill his glass.'

She had no choice but to obey. Picking up the

flagon again she took it to Pietro Gabrieli. As she bent forward to pour the wine he turned his head to look directly into her face. She felt acutely aware of him, the broad shoulders beneath the velvet doublet and the strong brown fingers holding the stem of his goblet towards her. Once more the hot colour flooded her cheeks and her hands began to shake. It was all she could do to hold the flagon steady until she had finished pouring the wine.

'Thank you.' The words were quietly said, yet with a hint of irony. Was he mocking her for having greeted him so haughtily in the yard? So, his tone seemed to imply, you are only a servant-girl after all!

Her master tapped his own glass. A little surprised, she refilled it. Normally Ercole was an abstemious drinker, preferring to keep his mind clear for business. She decided he must be finding the occasion something of a strain.

Pietro Gabrieli leaned forward to address Caterina. 'Tell me, madonna, are you fond of children?'

Caterina looked up at him, her eyes wide with apprehension. 'Children?' she repeated, almost in a whisper.

He went on hastily, 'I ask only because I'm hoping you may concern yourself with the welfare of my son Gentile.'

His *son*! Giulia stopped by the side-table on the pretext of rearranging some dishes so that she might eavesdrop on this fascinating conversation.

'Gentile is six years old,' Pietro continued. 'As you know, my wife died when he was born, so he has never known a mother's care. I fear he's been somewhat neglected during my absence.'

'Caterina adores children,' Monna Lucia

hastened to assure him. 'I've no doubt she'll make an excellent mother to your little boy.' She noticed Giulia still hovering near by and said sharply, 'That's all, girl. You may go.'

Giulia withdrew, her mind in a whirl. Of course they had known that Pietro Gabrieli was a widower, but she was certain no one had mentioned that he had a son. And, far from being fond of children, Caterina was inclined to be nervous of them. She always dreaded the visits of her young cousins, who played jokes on her and gave her the most fearful headache. It was Giulia who had to take them for walks in the town and play with them for hours in the garden.

And young Gentile Gabrieli, motherless since birth and neglected by his seafaring father, could well turn out to be yet another reason why Caterina should object to this unwelcome marriage.

Barely half-an-hour after the servants had finished clearing the dinner-table, Giulia was summoned to Caterina's chamber. She found her young mistress still dressed and seated before the mirror, staring unseeingly at her own reflection.

'Have you retired already, madonna?' Giulia asked in surprise.

'Messer Gabrieli must leave shortly for Padua,' Caterina said. 'He will spend the night there before embarking for Venice at first light.'

I was right to describe him as impatient, Giulia thought, if he cannot be bothered to take more than a cursory glance at his bride before returning posthaste to Venice!

She said curiously, 'But 'tis all arranged . . . The marriage plans are to go ahead?'

'He's with my father now, signing the contract.'

Caterina's shoulders drooped disconsolately. A note of despair entered her voice. 'It seems there's no escape.'

Giulia drew off the jewelled net to let Caterina's hair fall loose. She took up a hairbrush and began to apply it with slow, measured strokes. 'And when is the wedding to take place? Has a date been agreed?'

'As soon after Christmas as possible. Messer Gabrieli is busy preparing a fleet of merchant ships, and soon after we're wed he plans to sail for the Levant. Now that the trade routes are open again he wishes to make good use of them.'

A typical Venetian, Giulia reflected, obsessed with making money. Aloud she said, 'But Christmas is only two months hence. Your mother will want to return to Verona immediately to begin making arrangements.'

'Messer Gabrieli cannot spare the time to travel again to Verona,' Caterina said in the same flat tone. 'The wedding will be held at St Mark's church in Venice.'

'In *Venice*!' Giulia stopped brushing to stare at Caterina in the glass. 'But what does your father say to that?'

'Papa would say Yes to anything Messer Gabrieli suggested. They spent most of the time discussing some trade agreement that is to be drawn up between them. I believe they were more concerned with that than with the wedding.'

Giulia resumed her slow, regular brushing. Caterina's hair was fine as silk, a shade or so lighter than her own. Glancing at their two faces in the mirror, she thought that tonight they did not look in the least alike. The resemblance between them was a chance similarity of features and colouring, nothing more. Certainly in temperament they could hardly be more different.

She laid the brush aside and began undoing the tiny hooks that fastened Caterina's gown at the back. 'My, but this bodice is tight!' she remarked. 'I vow your bosom is becoming quite womanly. Still, I dare say Pietro Gabrieli will not object—so long as you don't grow too fat!'

Her attempt at humour fell on stony ground. Caterina said bitterly, 'I doubt if Pietro Gabrieli will notice if I'm fat or thin. He scarcely glanced in my direction all evening.'

'Didn't you have an opportunity to speak to him alone?'

Caterina stood up, allowing the dress to fall about her ankles. 'We walked in the loggia for a few minutes while Mama and Papa sat apart and pretended not to listen.'

'What did you talk about?'

'He told me of his house. It is known as the Ca' Gabrieli, for in Venice they're not allowed to call their houses palazzos, nor are their noblemen given titles. That would be against the laws of the Republic.'

Hardly a lover-like conversation! Giulia thought. 'What else?' she prompted.

'He gave me this ring.' Caterina held out her hand. On the third finger glowed a ruby set in a circle of small diamonds. 'And then he asked if he might kiss me, to seal the marriage contract.'

'And did you agree?' Giulia's eyes were suddenly bright with interest.

'I had no choice.' Caterina shuddered. 'It was horrible!'

'Why was it horrible?'

'Because he was not Bernardo!' Caterina pressed

both hands to her face as if the memory was too painful to bear. 'He asked me if there was something about his appearance that displeased me, since I seemed to find him so repugnant.'

Giulia gazed at her in fascination. 'And what did you say to that?'

'I told him I didn't like his beard.'

Giulia laughed. 'Poor man! I fear you've sent him away completely confused.' She picked up Caterina's discarded gown and folded it over her arm. 'At least he showed you some consideration. Perhaps he'll turn out to be not nearly so fearsome as he looks. Who knows, in time you may even come to love him as much as Bernardo!'

'Oh, Giulia!' Caterina turned on her furiously. ''Tis easy to see you've never been in love—You cannot possibly understand how I feel!' Still in her shift, she flung herself on the bed, sobbing wildly. 'I shall never love anyone but Bernardo . . . never!'

Giulia stared down at her, lost for words. In her heart she knew Caterina was right—she had never been in love. Oh, she had had more than her fair share of admirers, for hers were the kind of looks—that irresistible combination of golden hair and brown eyes, a full lower lip and rounded chin—that attracted men like bees to a honeypot. But most had been more interested in bedding her than wedding her, and none had shown that tender, loving regard she saw in Bernardo's eyes when he looked at Caterina. Was it because she lacked the qualities of character that could inspire so romantic a passion?

Or perhaps such elevated emotions were reserved exclusively for the rich and could never be the loss of a serving-maid like herself!

* * *

They returned to Verona on the following day, there being no further need to keep Caterina out of harm's way. Or, to be more exact, out of Bernardo's way. Now that Pietro Gabrieli had reappeared on the scene, the cabinet-maker's son was no longer regarded as a serious danger.

In the days that followed, Caterina hardly left her chamber. She seemed resigned, almost apathetic, as if she had given herself up to Fate and could offer no more resistance.

Fortunately Monna Lucia was too busy acquiring her daughter's trousseau to worry about her odd behaviour. Privately she grumbled about the inconvenience of holding the wedding in Venice and at a time of year which meant that few, if any, of their friends would be able to attend. In public, however, she lost no opportunity to inform her acquaintances that Caterina would be married from the Massimo house on the Grand Canal, the home of Pietro Gabrieli's married sister Francesca. The ceremony, of course, would be a quiet one, the bridegroom being a widower. Yet Caterina's dress was to be very fine, of cloth-of-gold with diamonds at the neck and waist.

It was during the final fitting for this gown, only three days before the wedding, that Monna Lucia made a shattering discovery.

'*Pregnant!*' She burst into her husband's office where he was engaged on the monthly accounts. 'Our daughter is pregnant by that good-for-nothing carpenter's son!'

Ercole Tebaldi smiled indulgently. 'You must be mistaken, my dear. Young girls are prone to these fancies.'

'I tell you this is no fancy, husband! She's four

months advanced and growing bigger by the minute!'

'But not big enough to show?' he said hopefully. 'The wedding-gown will surely disguise . . .'

'Are you suggesting we should try to delude Messer Gabrieli that the child is his, born four months premature?' Monna Lucia shot her husband a contemptuous look. '*You* may be a fool, Ercole, but he is not! I dread to think how angry he will be.'

Ercole turned white. Beads of sweat broke out across his brow and his hands began to shake. 'Leave me,' he said.

'Ercole, we must . . .'

'Did you not hear what I said, woman? *Leave me!*'

It was the first time in all their married life that he had dared to raise his voice to her. Monna Lucia was so taken by surprise that she allowed him to push her forcibly from the room and lock the door behind her.

An hour later he emerged, looking pale but resolute. 'I have a solution,' he declared. ''Tis a desperate remedy, but I believe it could work.' He opened the door and bellowed at a servant who happened to be passing. 'Tell Giulia I wish to see her—at once!'

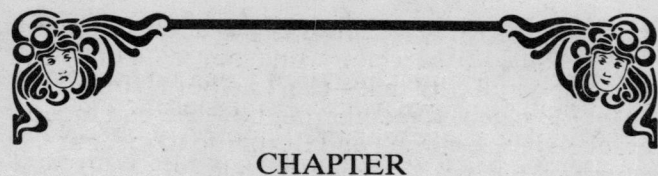

CHAPTER TWO

'You sent for me, sir?' Giulia asked apprehensively. She knew something was wrong and feared she was about to be blamed for it. Out of the corner of her eye she could see Monna Lucia sitting in a high-backed chair, her face set in a grim mask.

'Yes, child. Come in and close the door.' Ercole Tebaldi also seemed tense. When she came to stand before him, he stared into her face for a full ten seconds without speaking.

Giulia shifted uncomfortably, wondering if there was a smudge of dirt on her nose. To break the uneasy silence she said, 'I fear madonna Caterina is upset, sir. She's locked her door and will not . . .'

'It was *I* who locked Caterina's door,' Monna Lucia interrupted. 'And I've also taken the precaution of hiding the key where no one but myself can find it.'

Alarmed, Giulia looked at her master. His forehead was damp with sweat and his brown eyes shone with a strange luminosity.

'First let me ask you a question,' he said, speaking so quietly she had to lean forward to catch his words. 'Are you aware, Giulia, that my daughter is expecting a child?'

Before Giulia could attempt to answer, Monna Lucia snapped, 'What a ridiculous question! Of *course* she's aware of it, since it was she who connived at their meetings, no doubt standing guard outside the door while our daughter disported herself with that—that low-born scoundrel!'

Giulia paled, remembering how she had indeed arranged for Caterina and Bernardo to meet at the house of a candle-maker who had fallen on hard times and was only too glad to rent out his rooms by the hour.

'Look at her face! Can you not see she's guilty?'

'No, madonna!' Hot tears sprang into Giulia's eyes. 'I swear I didn't know your daughter is with child. She has confided nothing in me since—since she believes that I betrayed her. How I wish that she had!'

'Aye, so you could have tittle-tattled the news all over town!' Monna Lucia drew in a sharp breath. 'We must be thankful at least that no one else knows our shame . . . as yet.'

'No, nor *shall* know!' Ercole declared. He fixed Giulia with an intent look, speaking almost fiercely. 'What I'm about to say to you must go no further than this room, is that understood?'

'Yes, sir.'

'Naturally we cannot expect Pietro Gabrieli to accept Caterina as a suitable bride in her present condition,' he continued. 'None the less we shall leave for Venice tomorrow as arranged. That is, myself with my wife and daughter—and you, Giulia.'

She stared at him in astonishment. 'But if the wedding can no longer take place, then why are we . . . ?'

'The wedding *will* take place,' Ercole said resolutely. 'The first thing we shall do on arriving in Venice is to take Caterina to the Sisters of Mercy at the Convent of S. Cecilia. There she will stay, at least until she's had her child. Perhaps for ever. She's often expressed the desire to become a nun . . .'

'Only because she couldn't marry the man she loved!' Giulia burst out. 'But surely now you *must* let her marry Bernardo, for the sake of their child?'

'What?' Monna Lucia's voice shook with fury. 'Allow my daughter to marry the son of a cabinet-maker when all Verona knows she was betrothed to a nobleman? I could not live with the disgrace!' She turned her head away, her profile implacable.

'But I don't understand,' said Giulia, perplexed. 'If Caterina is to enter the convent . . . then how can there still be a wedding?'

Ercole looked at her gravely. 'Surely you must be aware how like Caterina you are? Your eyes, the shape of your face . . .'

'I will not listen to this!' Monna Lucia rose to her feet, her eyes flashing. ''Tis an insult to me and to my family. Nor will I play any part in this—this *infamous* masquerade. Indeed, I wash my hands of the whole affair.' She marched from the room, slamming the door behind her.

Ercole sighed. He turned to Giulia, who was gazing at him in bewilderment.

'Come and sit down,' he said, leading her to the chair Monna Lucia had just vacated. When she had perched herself uneasily on the edge, he pulled another chair closer and sat facing her. 'I'm about to tell you something that may shock you, Giulia. The truth is, my child, that the reason you so closely resemble Caterina is because you're her half-sister.' When Giulia made no visible response to this revelation, he added gently, 'I am your father, Giulia.'

A WEDDING IN VENICE

She nodded. 'Yes, I know. That is, I guessed as much.'

'You guessed?' He seemed genuinely amazed. How could he be so unaware of servants' gossip, Giulia wondered. He might be astute enough where money matters were concerned, but when it came to human beings he was sadly lacking in understanding.

Nevertheless he was her father. He had at last admitted it. She tried to see him through a daughter's eyes, but found it impossible. She had thought of him too long as a master.

'Yet you said nothing?' he persisted.

Giulia shrugged. 'It didn't trouble me. You treated me well, and I liked it better here than at the foundling hospital. Even though Monna Lucia . . .'

'Ah! She, I fear, has also guessed,' he admitted, looking embarrassed. 'Not that she's ever said it in so many words, but I'm aware that her manner to you is often less than kind.'

Giulia took a deep breath. 'May I ask, sir, who was my mother?'

A look of pain passed briefly over Ercole Tebaldi's face. 'I prefer not to speak of her. All you need know is that she was a woman of Venice.'

The colour drained from Giulia's cheeks. 'You mean she was a courtesan?'

He winced and for a moment was silent. Then he looked at her seriously. 'She was a woman of character, Giulia, and I loved her very much. Sometimes I've felt guilty for her sake that I could bring you here only as a servant, but there was no other way.' He bent forward, grasping her hands. 'Now I'm offering you the chance to lead a different life, as a mistress of a fine house, with beautiful clothes to wear and . . .'

Giulia said abruptly, 'You wish me to take Caterina's place?'

He nodded without speaking.

'But what of Pietro Gabrieli? Will he not object?'

'He needn't even know. Remember, he's met Caterina only once, two months ago, and then she hardly spoke to him. Once you're dressed accordingly, he'll accept you as Caterina, I'm certain of it.'

A sudden image of Pietro Gabrieli came into Giulia's mind . . . the dark, pointed beard and pale scar curving across his cheekbone. How could she hope to deceive such a man? He may not have looked closely at Caterina during his visit, but he had certainly subjected *her* to a most piercing scrutiny when she waited on him at dinner.

Moreover, he was undoubtedly aware that the Tebaldis had a maid-servant who bore a striking resemblance to his future bride.

She said unhappily, 'I must tell you, sir, that Messer Gabrieli . . .'

'Let me explain why this marriage is so important to me,' Ercole interrupted, speaking in a low, earnest voice. 'For some while I've wanted to expand my business by importing silks and gold thread from the East. Now the war is over, we can begin trading once more, but the Turks are wily fellows and will allow cargo to pass through their ports only at a high price. Pietro Gabrieli is known to have forged strong links with the Ottomans. They like and respect him. He's possibly the only man who can transport my cargoes without it costing me a king's ransom—and he's agreed to do so. That's why it's essential for me that this marriage should take place.'

'But, sir . . .'

'I am your father, Giulia!' Ercole rose to his feet, looking down at her with stern, reproachful eyes. 'And now you know the truth, you must surely acknowledge that you owe me a daughter's duty?'

Giulia hesitated. The idea of attempting to deceive Pietro Gabrieli was a daunting one; and yet at the same time she found it strangely exciting. She thought of that strange, handsome man who had spent so many years away from home, fighting for his city; and she thought of the six-year-old Gentile, who had never known a mother's love.

Finally, she thought of the alternative—a lifetime of drudgery spent at Monna Lucia's beck and call, with little or no chance of escape.

She raised her eyes to her father's eyes. 'I will do as you ask, sir. I will go to Venice . . . and take Caterina's place.'

A chill mist hung in the air as the barge carried them down-river from Padua, past townships and elegant villas, gardens and orange groves, towards the lagoon.

Ercole Tebaldi, grey-faced in the early morning light, sat beneath the canopy, his gaze fixed bleakly on the passing scene. Opposite him sat Giulia, huddled in a grey woollen cloak, and beside her a silent, red-eyed Caterina in a hooded mantle of dark green velvet edged with fur. Close by were stacked the wooden trunks containing Caterina's trousseau and her wedding-dress. Monna Lucia had refused to accompany them.

As they left the flat marshlands of the *Terra Firma* behind them, a wintry sun appeared in the sky, its weak light dispersing the mist to reveal a pattern of islands scattered about the lagoon.

Giulia left her seat to lean over the side, her spirits rising. Soon she would see Venice again, where she had spent the first seven years of her life, though heaven knows she could remember little about them save the hard beds and thin gruel of the foundling hospital. But still it was her birthplace and the home of her mother . . . that woman of Venice whom Ercole Tebaldi had once loved, if only briefly.

At last she was rewarded. Out of the water rose a city, shimmering in the hazy yellow light. From this distance it looked unreal, as dreamlike and insubstantial as a mirage. Giulia gazed at it entranced, watching it come nearer and nearer with every stroke of the oar.

At close quarters the city was far from dreamlike. All was noise and bustle, the waterways crowded with vessels of every shape and size, from flat-bottomed barges laden with fruit and vegetables to slow-moving merchant galleys.

They left the barge at the mouth of the Grand Canal, to continue their journey by gondola. Skilfully their boatman wielded his single oar, the high curved prow of his narrow craft cutting fast through the murky waters of the canal. Caterina shared the cabin's double seat with her father while Giulia sat opposite, fascinated by the painted façades of the houses and the oriental splendour of the churches with their golden domes and minarets. It seemed almost an Eastern city, haunting and mysterious, and she felt a delicious thrill of anticipation.

When they arrived at the Convent of S. Cecilia, Ercole Tebaldi helped both girls from the gondola and ordered the boatman to wait. They climbed the steps to a thick, iron-studded door set in a high wall. Ercole pulled the bell-rope.

After some minutes a nun slid back the grille to inquire their business. Ercole gave his name and requested an audience with the Prioress. The nun closed the grille and there was a further delay while she pulled back the heavy bolts before the door swung open.

They were taken to a huge, vaulted chamber, unfurnished except for a number of magnificent oil-paintings depicting scenes from the Old Testament. The nun beckoned Ercole to follow her. Grim-faced he went, leaving the two girls alone.

It seemed very dark and cold after the noisy brilliance of the city outside. Giulia glanced uneasily at Caterina and saw to her alarm that she was close to fainting. 'Madonna, you are ill!' She helped Caterina to a stone window-seat and knelt beside her, chafing her hands. 'Listen to me,' she said urgently, her voice echoing round the empty room. 'If you don't wish to stay here after your baby is born, no one can make you! Oh, your mother's angry now, but in time she'll relent. She'll take you back.'

Caterina shook her head. 'I can never return to Verona; my father has told me so. I must stay here for the rest of my life. There's nowhere else I can go.'

Giulia said impatiently, 'Oh, you're taking it all too meekly! Why won't you *fight* for what you want?'

Caterina leant her head against the stone casement. 'I no longer have the strength to fight,' she sighed. 'And if I cannot marry Bernardo then I'd sooner become a nun than be forced to marry someone else.'

Giulia stared at her, feeling helpless. She saw that Caterina was far too occupied with her present misery to care what happened to her. But after a while, when her child had been born and she regained her natural strength, surely then she would want to return to the outside world and pick up the threads of her life once more?

The door opened and Ercole returned, accompanied by a tall nun with a calm, handsome face.

'This is Mother Maria Innocenti, the Prioress of this convent,' he said. 'I've told her everything and she's agreed to help us.' He was looking almost cheerful, as if a great weight had been lifted off his back. Raising Caterina from the window-seat, he kissed her fondly on both cheeks. 'Go with her, my dear. She will take care of you. And I'll come to visit you often, whenever I'm in Venice.'

As if in a trance Caterina walked across the room to stand before Mother Maria, her head bowed. The Prioress regarded her impassively; then her gaze travelled to Giulia. 'Both girls must come with me,' she said, 'if we're to effect this substitution.'

Giulia's heart was pounding as they followed the Prioress along the corridor to a small white-walled cell. Here they were instructed to undress.

When they stood naked and shivering before her, Mother Maria told them to exchange clothes. 'By the time you leave this room,' she said calmly, 'Caterina will have become Giulia . . . and Giulia Caterina.'

Caterina was the first to obey, pulling on the coarse homespun garments almost eagerly in her haste to cover her already swollen belly.

Giulia dressed more slowly. The silken undergarments felt strange against her skin, the gown heavier and more cumbersome than she was used to. Finally she donned the velvet mantle, her hands caressing the soft fur. She suddenly became aware that the Prioress was watching her, and flushed.

'You've forgotten the ring,' said Mother Maria.

Caterina took off Pietro Gabrieli's betrothal ring and handed it to Giulia. 'Take it, with my blessing,' she said bitterly. 'Heaven knows I'm glad to be rid of it!'

Giulia slipped the ring on to her finger. It fitted perfectly, whereas on Caterina it had been a little loose. Was this an omen? she wondered.

Mother Maria summoned another nun to take Caterina to the chapel so that she might spend some time in prayer and meditation. She went without a backward glance or even a word of farewell.

Giulia turned unhappily to the Prioress. 'Do you think that what I'm doing is sinful?' she asked. 'Am I wrong to take part in this deception?'

The nun regarded her with cool detachment. 'Deception can take many forms, my child. If you intend to fulfil your part honestly—to love and obey this man you are to marry—then I don't think you need regard what you're doing as sinful.'

Giulia thought of Pietro Gabrieli. It would be easy to love and obey such a husband, she decided. 'I shall deal with him as honestly as I can,' she said. 'Perhaps more honestly than Caterina, for *I* am not in love with someone else.'

For a brief second something flickered in Mother Maria's sombre dark eyes, but still she did not smile. 'Your father's right,' she said. 'In looks you're amazingly like your half-sister. In character, however . . . Well, perhaps Pietro Gabrieli may not be getting such a bad bargain after all.'

And with this surprising statement she turned and swept through the door, leaving Giulia to follow.

When they re-entered the reception chamber, Ercole gave a slight but perceptible start. 'Incredible,' he murmured as his gaze alightened on Giulia. 'There *is* a difference, of course . . . but it would be apparent only to someone who knows you both well.' He turned to the Prioress. 'Well, what do you think of her?'

'Giulia already knows what I think,' replied the nun. 'And now 'tis time for you to be on your way.'

The heavy door clanged shut behind them, and Giulia's thoughts were all of Caterina, left imprisoned behind those high, forbidding walls.

But as she walked down the steps to the waiting gondola, her skirts swishing about her ankles, it seemed as though she had indeed acquired a new identity. When the boatman held out his hand to assist her she accepted with a gracious smile, and if he wondered why two girls had entered the convent and only one emerged, he no doubt assumed that it was the maid-servant who had stayed behind.

Francesca Massimo received them in the vast, mosaic-floored portego of her husband's mansion close by the Ponte di Rialto. She was a small, vivacious woman who bore not the least resemblance to her brother Pietro, partly because her hair had been lightened from its natural dark brown to a bright, fashionable yellow.

'My wife is desolate she cannot attend the wedding,' Ercole was quick to explain. 'But she fell sick two days ago and the fever was running too high for her to think of making such a journey.'

Francesca expressed her sympathy. 'Be assured I will give Caterina all the help and support I can,' she said warmly. 'After all, tomorrow will be the most important day of her life.'

Giulia, keeping her eyes cast down, murmured her thanks.

'I'm afraid my daughter is exhausted,' Ercole apologised. 'Perhaps it would be best if she retired for the rest of the day.'

Francesca looked disappointed. 'Oh, but I'd arranged a small dinner party. Just a few friends . . .'

'She's not hungry,' said Ercole. 'And I think she should rest.'

Giulia thought, *He's afraid I shall give myself away even before the wedding has taken place.*

'I understand. Come, Caterina—I will show you to your room.' Francesca led her up a grand, curving staircase. 'Your trunks have already been sent on to the Ca' Gabrieli—except that containing your wedding-dress, of course!'

She flung open the door into a large chamber with a painted ceiling and damasked walls. On a dais stood a bed hung with brocade and tasselled in gold. Giulia, unused to such luxury, could not restrain a gasp.

'Is something wrong?' Francesca was looking at her anxiously.

'No . . . No, of course not. 'Tis just that everything seems so strange and new.'

'You poor child!' Francesca spoke with genuine sympathy. 'I fear the first few months of married life are never easy for a girl, especially when she's a long way from her home and family. Caterina, I hope you will think of me as your friend?'

Giulia took her courage in both hands. 'Francesca, will you please tell me something of Pietro's family? He—he said so little when he came to our house.' The lies were beginning to trip more easily off her tongue. She added hastily, 'I know there is Gentile, of course. Pietro said he was particularly anxious for me to take an interest in his son's upbringing.'

Francesca sighed. 'Ah, Gentile! I fear the poor child has become something of a bone of contention.'

'Between whom?' Giulia asked, surprised.

'Between his father and the Benettis, his mother's family. *They* would take him over completely if they could, but of course Pietro will not allow it.' She settled down in a carved chair as if preparing for a lengthy gossip. 'You'll find it a very masculine household, I'm afraid. Apart from Pietro and his son Gentile, there's my younger brother Alessandro, who I'm sure will welcome you with open arms, for he's inordinately fond of pretty women.'

'Is he not married?'

'Sweet heaven, no!' Francesca stared at her in amazement. 'Are you not acquainted with the Republic's hereditary laws? In Venice, property is bequeathed to all surviving sons jointly, so 'tis accepted that only one brother shall marry, otherwise a family's fortunes would be dispersed beyond recall.'

'I see.' Giulia felt a pang of sympathy for Alessandro. If he was so fond of pretty women it seemed hard he must remain a bachelor for the sake of his brother's child.

Francesca put her head on one side like a curious bird, her eyes bright with amusement. 'I must say, Caterina, you're not at all how I expected.'

'In what way?' Giulia asked, alarmed.

'Well, for one thing you're far more beautiful than Pietro led me to believe. But he also said . . .' Francesca broke off.

Giulia's heart missed a beat. 'What did he say?'

'Heavens, I really must guard my tongue! My husband always tells me I speak without thinking.' Leaning forward, she continued confidentially, 'But you must know that Pietro's views on women have been influenced by the years he has spent in the East. When he told me you were exactly the kind of wife he required, well, frankly I imagined you as rather meek-natured and lacking in spirit.'

Giulia thought of how Caterina had behaved when Pietro Gabrieli came to visit them, and was not surprised he had formed such a view of her. 'I—I was unwell at the time,' she said. 'I fear he may not have seen me as I truly am.'

'Oh, my dear, don't apologise!' Francesca laughed. 'I'm delighted, for Pietro can be very domineering when he chooses and it isn't always good for him to have his own way.'

Giulia said slowly, 'When he came to our house in the country he brought with him a Turkish servant . . . a giant of a man who had lost his tongue.'

Francesca nodded. 'Kasim. And he's not the only oddity you'll find at the Ca' Gabrieli, I warn you. Indeed, Pietro's marked preference for all things oriental is earning him an unfortunate reputation. People think he has come back from the wars a barbarian and therefore cannot be trusted . . .' She caught sight of Giulia's travel-weary face and rose to her feet. 'But I've kept you talking long enough. Your father wished you to get some rest before the excitement of tomorrow. I will send up a cold collation to your room.' She kissed Giulia's cheek. 'I'm glad you're to be my sister-in-law, Caterina, for I believe you will make Pietro an excellent wife—perhaps even better than he deserves.'

When she had gone, Giulia opened the shutters. Her room looked out on to the Ponte di Rialto, its wooden drawbridge raised to admit a fleet of round-ships carrying freight, while on the quayside below her hucksters were hawking fruit and fish, their voices mingling with the cries of gondoliers plying their vessels along the crowded waterway.

Her senses reeled with the sights and sounds of Venice. This was her city! She had come home at last . . . and for the moment could only rejoice at her good fortune, suppressing all doubts and fears as to what the morrow might bring.

The cavernous interior of St Mark's church seemed almost pagan in its splendour. A glittering treasure-house of riches plundered from Byzantium, ablaze with gold and precious stones in the light of a thousand glittering candles, its magnificence all but took Giulia's breath away. As she walked with her father up the aisle to the chapel of S. Clement she began to shake.

Ercole must have sensed her nervousness, for he pressed her hand against his side and whispered, 'Courage! And remember, when the priest asks for your name tell him Caterina Giulia Tebaldi. That will ensure you're truly married, in your own right.'

So he was at last acknowledging her as his daughter, Giulia realised; but she could take no joy in it, for all her attention was riveted on the solitary figure of Pietro Gabrieli standing before the altar. As he turned to watch her approach she hastily lowered her eyes to the ground, but not before she had caught sight of the small knot of people awaiting them.

Aware of their scrutiny, she took comfort in the knowledge that at least she looked the part. The cloth-of-gold wedding-gown fitted her almost perfectly, the low-cut bodice moulding her figure to the hips while the skirt fell in graceful folds to a long train at the back. Her blonde hair, dressed that morning by Francesca's maid, was braided on top of her head and covered by a veil of patterned gauze. She was thankful, as she joined Pietro Gabrieli at the altar, that her face was hidden from his gaze.

Afterwards she could remember little of the ceremony, except that she had given her name as Ercole instructed in a voice that surprised even herself by its firmness and clarity.

When the priest pronounced them man and wife, Pietro turned to lift the veil so that he might look for the first time into her face. Unwillingly she raised her eyes to meet his, half-expecting to see him shocked at the realisation she was not Caterina.

Instead it was she who received the shock.

'You've shaved off your beard!' she exclaimed before she could stop herself.

'You told me you didn't like it,' he said gravely. 'I trust you find my appearance improved by its removal?'

'Why, yes . . .' she stammered, thinking he looked handsomer than ever now that the well-shaped mouth and strong lines of his jaw were revealed.

He smiled. 'In that case perhaps you won't object—this time—when I kiss you?'

Before she could say a word he bent his head to press his lips to hers and kept them there for a long moment, as if to test her reaction. She stood immobile, dimly aware of a subdued murmur of approval from the small congregation, but more acutely conscious of her own wildly-beating heart and the treacherous trembling of her lips beneath his.

At length he raised his head to give her a questioning look. Giulia, blushing, found herself unable to tear her eyes away from his. It was the priest who broke the spell, clearing his throat to suggest they proceed with the nuptial Mass.

As she knelt at the altar-rail, Giulia recovered at least some of her composure. The first hurdle was over, she told herself. He had accepted her as Caterina and now she had only to be careful not to give herself away. How fortunate that she had shared so much of Caterina's education and upbringing! Though not born a lady, she could put on a convincing enough performance to fool most people.

But as her thoughts quietened and the words of the Mass began to penetrate her brain, she remembered the calm face of the Prioress and heard her quiet voice . . . *'If you intend to fulfil your part honestly—to love and obey this man you are to marry—then I don't think you need regard what you're doing as sinful.'*

Giulia was filled with remorse. How could she have thought in terms of fooling people and putting on a performance? Closing her eyes, she prayed in earnest that she might prove a good wife to Pietro Gabrieli and a loving mother to his little son.

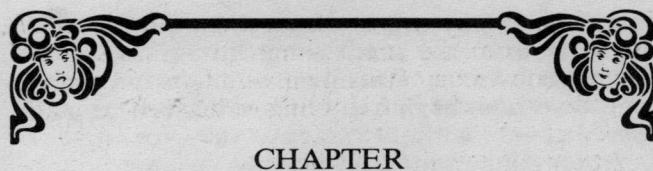

CHAPTER THREE

THE WEDDING party emerged from the dark interior of the church to find the broad expanse of St Mark's Square fast filling up with booths and sideshows in readiness for the Carnival due to start on the morrow, on Twelfth Night. Somehow the word had spread that there was a wedding taking place in the Doge's church, and a small crowd had gathered outside from curiosity. When they recognised Pietro Gabrieli there was a sudden surge of interest, and the bridal procession was riotously pursued across the piazzetta by the good-humoured citizens of Venice, already in carnival mood.

On the quayside Giulia was helped into the waiting gondola by so many pairs of eager hands that she began to laugh, and she was still smiling and waving happily when the boatman steered his craft away from the jetty.

'I'd forgotten that tomorrow is Carnival!' she exclaimed. 'No wonder everyone's in such excellent spirits.'

She turned to find Pietro watching her intently. 'I fear you may find Venice noisy in the next few weeks,' he said. 'But there's no need for you to venture abroad in the city if you don't wish.'

Giulia was about to say there was nothing she would like better than to venture abroad at

Carnival time, but she managed to bite back the words before they reached her lips. Heavens! she thought, it will be difficult enough to play Caterina as it is without having to be Caterina as he remembered her—pallid-faced and sick for love of another man.

After a few minutes she became aware that their gondola was stationary, rocking gently in the middle of the canal, the boatman leaning on his pole. She looked at Pietro in surprise. 'Is something wrong?'

'We're waiting for our guests to go first,' he explained. 'Naturally they want to arrive at the Ca' Gabrieli before us, so that they can be there to welcome you.'

Giulia nodded. She felt very conscious of their isolation, shielded from the public gaze by the curtains enclosing the small cabin. The double seat was by no means spacious, so they were forced to sit close together. Even through the thick stuff of her gown she could feel the warmth of Pietro's thigh against her own.

Nervously she said, 'I did not see your son—Gentile—in the church.'

'No, he stayed at home with his aunt.'

'I—I'm looking forward to meeting him.'

'You'll see him soon enough.' His tone was dismissive, as if the subject bored him. She recalled Francesca's remark that Gentile had become a bone of contention between his father and the Benetti family. Was this aunt a relation of Pietro's first wife, she wondered.

Before she could summon the courage to put the question, he said abruptly, 'Your mother was not at the ceremony. Why was that?'

Giulia had completely forgotten about Monna

Lucia. She tried to infuse some feeling into her voice. 'Alas, she developed a fever and couldn't make the journey to Venice. She—she was heart-broken she could not attend.'

'No doubt,' he observed in a dry tone.

'But my father said you wouldn't wish to postpone the wedding, since you must sail in a week or so for the Levant.'

'That's true.' His eyes rested thoughtfully on her face. 'I hope you won't mind me leaving you so soon, Caterina?'

Giulia shook her head. 'I know you're a seafaring man, my lord, and must often be away from home for many weeks.'

Surely that was as meek an answer as he could wish, she thought.

'I'm glad to see you looking in better health than when last we met,' he said conversationally.

Giulia cast down her eyes. 'I—I fear I was a trifle indisposed on that occasion.'

'Perhaps you were also feeling nervous at the prospect of meeting your future husband?' His voice was gentle. 'It would be quite understandable in the circumstances.'

Giulia was beginning almost to enjoy her rôle. ''Tis true, my lord,' she murmured. 'I confess I *was* a little nervous.'

'And no doubt that would account for your somewhat violent reaction to my beard?'

Giulia raised her eyes to his face, smiling shyly. 'I'm sorry if I offended you, my lord. But the beard did give you a rather . . . sinister appearance.'

'You don't find me sinister now, I trust?'

Gravely she regarded his lean, arrogant face with the disfiguring scar. The well-shaped mouth clearly revealed by the absence of beard held a suggestion of sensuality in the curved lower lip and there was a gleam in his dark eyes that warned her she must not relax her guard for an instant. 'No, not sinister,' she said slowly. 'But still a little frightening, I must admit.'

He slid an arm along the back of her seat, moving even closer within the cramped confines of the cabin. 'Don't be afraid, Caterina. You'll find me the most considerate of husbands, I promise. I would not dream of using cruelly such beauty, such innocence . . .' His free hand caressed her neck before moving lightly, almost experimentally, over the rounded breasts pushed upwards by the stomacher of her gown.

Giulia's heart began to pound alarmingly. At his touch a sudden fire had begun to surge through her body as though a fuse had been lit somewhere deep within her. Yet once again she had the impression he was putting her to the test. Those watchful eyes had never once left her face, and she feared they must surely detect the signs of dizzying weakness that swept over her as his hand grew bolder still, sliding inside her low-cut bodice.

With a gasp she moved away so abruptly that the gondola rocked from side to side and she was forced to clutch at the sides. 'This vessel seems a trifle unsteady, my lord,' she stammered, to cover her confusion.

'You're right.' He relaxed, withdrawing his arm and leaning back in his seat. 'Far better to wait until tonight, when we shall find ourselves in more stable surroundings.'

He sounded content, she thought, as though reassured by the modesty of her demeanour. Yet, if he had but known it, the feelings he aroused in her were anything but modest! Hot colour flooded her cheeks at the recollection and she turned her face away, pretending to stare into the water.

He rapped out an order to the boatman and they began to move forward. Giulia let out a sigh of relief.

Yet if she feared to be alone with her husband now, in the comparative safety of a gondola, how much more difficult would it be tonight, in the seclusion of their marriage-bed?

Fortunately these disquieting thoughts were driven from her mind by their arrival at the Ca' Gabrieli. Her first sight of its impressive façade, with its ornate balconies and soaring fluted columns, filled her with awe. Was this truly to be her home? How could she—born in the foundling hospital and brought up in servitude—dare to play the rôle of mistress in so magnificent a house?

The boatman tied his gondola to a mooring-post painted in armorial stripes of black and scarlet— the Gabrieli colours, Giulia thought, remembering that Pietro when first she saw him had been clad in black and scarlet.

Kasim awaited them on the steps, his massive bulk clothed in a wide-sleeved robe and with a snow-white turban on his head. He bowed without smiling and held out a hand to assist her from the rocking vessel. In her nervousness Giulia stumbled over her train, but found herself firmly held by the Turk's strong arm. 'Thank you, Kasim,' she murmured, and in the next instant felt Pietro's lighter touch at her elbow, guiding her towards the entrance.

The main hall, at water level, was paved with diagonal squares of white Istrian stone and red-veined marble. From there they climbed the stairs past the mezzanine floor to the portego, a long gallery lined on one side with tall windows looking on to the canal. Tables were laid out here, laden with dishes—roast capon, goose, pheasant, sweetbreads in wine and gilded fruit. As they entered the room, a group of musicians struck up a tune and conversation abruptly ceased, all eyes turning to stare at the bride with frank curiosity.

'Caterina!' Francesca hurried forward to embrace her. Dressed in a gown so profusely adorned with flashing gems as almost to outshine the bride, she was none the less generous in her praise of Giulia's appearance. 'My dear, you look so lovely I could weep! And how fortunate you are to have hair that is naturally blonde—why, in colouring one might take you for a Venetian born and bred! Now, let me present you to our guests . . .'

At first Giulia was tense, fearful of betraying herself by a word or gesture, and her nervousness was not helped by the hovering presence of Ercole Tebaldi, anxiously watching her every move. Once the feasting was over, however, she was at least saved the attention of her husband, who wandered off to mingle with the more important guests, among them several senators in their red damask togas. It was left to Francesca to introduce her to a confusing number of friends and relations, among them Francesca's own husband, who to Giulia's astonishment was at least sixty and so afflicted with rheumatism he could walk only with a stick. Though plainly fond of Francesca, he seemed to treat her more as a daughter than a wife. A strange marriage, Giulia thought; but perhaps no stranger than her own.

'And what of me, sweet Sister?' A slender young man with long dark hair appeared beside them, swaying slightly and suspiciously bright-eyed. 'Am I not worthy to be introduced?'

'Alessandro, at last!' Francesca turned to her brother reproachfully. 'Where have you been?'

'Drowning my sorrows. Weddings always make me feel horribly depressed. But now I've come to pay my respects to our new sister-in-law.' He swept Giulia a none-too-steady bow; then, straightening, looked at her with open admiration. 'By heaven, but you're a beauty! What can Pietro have done to deserve such luck!'

His impudence brought a flush to Giulia's cheek, but he was so good-looking, with a smooth olive complexion and striking light green eyes, that she could well understand that he must find his state of enforced celibacy irksome, to say the least. Small wonder if he resented Pietro's freedom to marry and have children!

She smiled at him. 'I'm glad to meet you, Alessandro. When Pietro sets sail in a few days' time there will doubtless be many matters on which I shall need your advice.'

He stared at her, then slowly smiled. When he spoke again it was with a disarming candour. 'There's nothing that would give me greater pleasure, Caterina, than to be your friend.' He took her arm, leading her aside. 'Tell me everything you want to know.'

After a moment's hesitation she said frankly, 'Well, first, there's the matter of Pietro's son. I was hoping he'd be here, at the marriage feast, for I'm sure he must be as anxious to meet me as I am to meet him.'

'You want to meet Gentile?' He took the empty goblet from her hand and set it down on the table. 'Then come with me.'

'Now? But should I not . . . ?'

'Come with me,' he repeated, taking her by the hand.

She cast an uncertain glance at Pietro and saw that he was not even looking in her direction. A little reluctantly she allowed Alessandro to lead her up the stairs to the floor above.

They entered a modest suite of rooms. Alessandro knocked on an inner door and waited until an imperious female voice bade them enter.

The room was sparsely furnished. A hatchet-faced woman of uncertain age sat by the window, stitching at her embroidery. Beside her a small boy was hunched over a desk, writing laboriously.

'Please excuse us for intruding, Monna Clarissa,' Alessandro said with an air of assumed deference, 'but my new sister-in-law has expressed a wish to meet her stepson.'

The woman rose to her feet, staring at Giulia. For a brief second, naked hostility flared in her eyes before she stiffly bowed her head. 'We are honoured, madonna,' she murmured.

'Come here, Gentile,' ordered Alessandro, 'and greet your stepmother.'

Obediently the little boy slipped from his chair and came to stand before them, gazing up at Giulia with huge, solemn eyes. She caught her breath, for he was a miniature replica of his father, though far too thin and white-faced. Impulsively she knelt beside him so that her eyes were on a level with his. 'Would you like to come downstairs, Gentile?' she asked. 'There's music . . . and plenty of sugar-sweets to eat.'

He said nothing, but continued to stare at her as if she had spoken in a foreign language.

'His uncle would prefer him to remain at his

studies.' Monna Clarissa's voice was tight with disapproval.

'His uncle?' Straightening, Giulia looked at Alessandro in bewilderment.

'Not me!' He grinned at her. 'Monna Clarissa is referring to Gentile's *maternal* uncle, Cardinal Benetti.'

'Cardinal Lorenzo Benetti,' the woman supplied, speaking his name as proudly as if she referred to the Holy Father himself. 'My nephew.'

So Monna Clarissa was *great*-aunt to Gentile! No wonder she was so advanced in years—hardly a lively companion for a boy of his age, Giulia thought.

She said firmly, 'Well, Gentile's *father* wishes him to come to the feast.' She knew that Pietro probably wished nothing of the sort, but there was something in Monna Clarissa's manner that made her determined not to be intimidated. She held out her hand to Gentile. 'Come, we'll go downstairs.'

Trustingly he slipped his thin white hand into hers and she led him from the room.

As they descended the stairs Alessandro muttered, 'Bravo! You've won a significant victory—and earned yourself an enemy, I fear.' When she looked at him in alarm, he added, 'Oh, don't worry! The Benettis dislike us all on principle. Monna Clarissa would be your enemy anyway, merely because you've married a Gabrieli.'

'Then why does Pietro entrust his son to her?'

He shrugged. 'Perhaps because he's had no choice, until now.'

With Gentile's hand clasped in hers she entered the portego. There was a momentary hush as the little boy appeared and she felt him hang back fearfully, but she bent to whisper, 'Would you like an orange?'

He nodded silently and allowed her to draw him further into the room. She filled a dish with segments of fruit dipped in sugar and gave it to him. Very slowly he picked out one and put it into his mouth. A look of pure bliss spread over his face and Giulia laughed.

But when she turned to share the joke with Alessandro, she found that his place at her side had been taken by Pietro, whose expression was so ominous that her smile froze on her lips.

Before either of them could speak, however, there came a crash. Gentile had dropped the dish, spilling sugared fruits at their feet. The little boy seemed transfixed with horror, then he raised frightened eyes to Pietro's face and with a shriek threw himself against Giulia's skirt.

She put a hand on his quivering shoulders. *He's terrified of his father!*, she thought, and the realisation strengthened her own resolve. 'I was eager to make Gentile's acquaintance,' she explained. 'It seemed a shame for him not to take part in our celebrations.'

Pietro's lips compressed into a thin line but he was prevented from speaking freely by the small crowd that had gathered round them, drawn by the noise of the crash.

Giulia added in a low voice, so that only he could hear, 'After all, you did ask me to take a particular interest in your son.'

He said grudgingly, 'So I did. However, the child isn't used to mixing with people. He'd be happier upstairs.' Turning from her, he summoned a servant to take the boy away and another to clear up the mess from the floor.

As Gentile was dragged from her skirts, Giulia was overcome with pity for the stricken-faced little boy. Calling to the servant to wait, she put a fresh peach into Gentile's hand and smiled at him, murmuring, 'I'll come to see you again soon, never fear.' But he gave no sign that he was pleased at the prospect, or had even understood what she said.

Giulia turned to her husband. 'I'm sorry if I acted thoughtlessly, my lord. I should have consulted you first, before I . . .'

'Nonsense!' It was Francesca who interrupted, smiling gaily. 'You did absolutely right, my dear. That poor child leads a miserable existence with only the gaunt-faced Benetti woman for company, and if you can bring some happiness into his life then Pietro should be delighted.' Teasingly she prodded his chest. 'You're a lucky man, and I hope you'll treat your wife with the respect she deserves. She's not one of your Eastern slaves, you know!'

It was clear that Pietro was far from amused by this remark. Unabashed, Francesca ordered the musicians to play so that the dancing might begin. 'The bride and groom must lead the way,' she announced in a carrying voice, 'and the rest of us will follow.'

Giulia trod a stately measure with her husband in complete silence. When it was finished he bowed politely and went off to talk to her father, whereupon her hand was claimed by Alessandro. From that moment on she danced frequently with her brother-in-law and the other guests, but not again with her husband.

Later in the evening Ercole came to bid her goodbye. She said pleadingly, 'You will come to see me, when you're next in Venice?'

'Of course, my dear.' On the pretext of kissing

her cheek, he bent close to murmur. 'You've done well . . . but I beg you to be careful. Bringing the child downstairs—that was too bold. You cannot afford to take such risks.'

She realised with dismay that once again she had not behaved as Caterina would have down in the circumstances. 'You don't think anyone suspects . . . ?'

Ercole shook his head. 'But you must be on your guard. And whatever you do, make no attempt to visit Caterina. That would be foolhardy.'

She agreed, though reluctantly. The thought of Caterina locked away behind those high stone walls made her feel strangely guilty, almost as if she were to blame for what had happened.

But when Ercole had gone, and she turned back into the room now filled with merriment, she decided that her half-sister would not for an instant wish to change places with her. On the contrary, Caterina would find the peaceful atmosphere of the convent, where she was free to dream of Bernardo and their unborn child, far preferable to this roomful of strangers with their wine-flushed faces and noisy laughter.

Alessandro seized her round the waist and whirled her back into the dancing, holding her much too tightly for a brotherly embrace. Out of the corner of her eye she saw that Pietro was watching them, and she tried to draw back, but Alessandro only laughed. 'Are you afraid to make him jealous?' he teased. ''Twill only serve to increase his ardour, I promise you.' Pulling her close again, despite her resistance, he whispered softly, 'Though I fear his ardour will be nothing compared to what I am feeling at this moment . . .'

Giulia blushed hotly, wishing she could escape.

Every minute carried her nearer to the time when she must carry her deception through to its logical conclusion. The revelry around her, Alessandro's too-obvious attentions—everything conspired to make her feel more isolated than ever now that Ercole had gone, abandoning her to her fate.

'My dear, you're beginning to look weary.' Francesca appeared at her side. ''Tis time you retired.'

Giulia allowed her sister-in-law to lead her from the room. A chorus of cheers and lewd remarks followed them, but she paid no heed.

Francesca opened the door into a large bed-chamber. 'Pietro had this room specially prepared for you,' she said, adding in an odd tone, 'I only hope you approve of his taste.'

Giulia stared about her. The walls were hung with tapestries woven in an intricate oriental design, the floor covered with thick rugs, and the bed half-hidden beneath a canopy of swathed white silk. On a dais by the window stood a divan upholstered in gold brocade and strewn with cushions. A strange musky perfume hung in the air.

'Ay, you might well imagine yourself in some Turkish harem,' Francesca said ironically, watching her face. 'Especially when you see the maidservant Pietro has given you.' She clapped her hands.

From a cunningly concealed door in the wall appeared a young girl clad in pale green draperies with gold bangles around her slim brown wrists and ankles. She came to stand before Giulia with eyes downcast, the rest of her face hidden behind a veil.

'Zoe understands a little of our language, although she doesn't care to speak it.' Francesca turned to the girl. 'Attend your mistress. She wishes to prepare for bed.'

When she had gone, Zoe beckoned Giulia to follow her through the concealed door. It led into a small room tiled in marble with a sunken bath. Giulia had heard about the strange eastern custom of immersing oneself totally in water, but she had never before seen such a thing in a private house, nor dreamt that she would be expected to venture into one. With some trepidation she allowed the girl to undress her and help her into the warm, scented water. To her surprise she found it a curiously pleasant sensation. Gradually the tension in her limbs seemed to ebb away, leaving her calm and relaxed.

When she emerged from the bath, Zoe dried her with a soft towel before smoothing perfumed oils into her skin. Finally she slipped a robe over her mistress's head—and Giulia came to her senses with a start.

For she was certain that this loose silken robe, of so fine a texture as to be almost transparent, could not possibly have been part of Caterina's trousseau. Monna Lucia would never dream of choosing such an exotic garment for her daughter to wear, not even on her wedding night. Giulia tried to protest, but Zoe only shook her head and gestured for her to return to the bedchamber.

Helplessly Giulia slipped between the sheets, her mind busy with speculation. Had Pietro chosen this robe himself . . . brought it back from the Orient for his bride? Was it her husband's intention to turn her into a slave-girl, passively obedient like the beautiful Zoe? She lay stiffly in the soft, luxurious bed, staring up at the tent-like draperies above her and feeling more and more as though she had

A WEDDING IN VENICE

stumbled into some Turkish sultan's seraglio.

The door swung open with a bang. Giulia hastily drew the sheet up to her chin as the wedding guests burst into the room, laughing and singing. Tall among them was Pietro, in a fur-trimmed robe open to the waist, his expression proud but withdrawn. He allowed himself to be pushed towards the bed, but when the guests in their enthusiasm would have gone further, he turned in sudden anger and ordered them from the room.

There were cries of 'Shame!' Francesca pushed her way to the front, holding something aloft. 'The ring, Pietro—don't forget the ring!'

He took the simple gold band from his sister and placed it carefully on a carved table beside the bed. Giulia knew well enough its significance, for this was the ring of approval given to a bride by her husband when their marriage had been consummated, to show that he was pleased with her.

Suddenly there was a loud explosion outside the window and for an instant the room was filled with flaring light.

' 'Tis midnight! Carnival has begun . . .'

With a whoop the guests left the room to join the revellers outside, the fun of a wedding night overshadowed by the greater excitement of the Carnival.

As Pietro closed the door behind them Giulia drew a long, shuddering breath. He returned to stand by the bed, gazing down at her without expression. Then, with a swift movement that took her by surprise, he jerked the sheet from her hand and pulled it back to expose her trembling body in the silken shift.

For a long moment he surveyed her in silence, his eyes lingering on the high pointed breasts and curving hips clearly visible through the filmy silk. 'So beautiful,' he murmured, half to himself. 'I hadn't expected to find such beauty in a wife . . .'

Then he saw that her eyes were wide with apprehension, and in an instant his mood seemed to change. He sat down on the edge of the bed, gently taking hold of her wrist. 'Caterina, are you still afraid of me?'

With difficulty Giulia found her voice. 'No, my lord—I'm not afraid.' But she was certain his fingers must have found her racing pulse.

'At one time I feared . . .' He broke off, frowning as if perplexed, then slowly bent to press his lips to hers in a tender, reverent kiss.

Giulia was astonished that he should be capable of such restraint, but almost at once the fire he had already lit within her sprang once more into life. Involuntarily her lips parted beneath his, soft and inviting. For a brief moment he seemed startled by her response, then recovered swiftly to take possession of her mouth with a fierce, demanding hunger he could no longer keep in check. Giulia clung to him, forgetting her fears in the tide of passion sweeping over them both and knowing only that here at last was the one man to whom she could give herself unstintingly, with all the generosity of her ardent nature.

Unerringly his hands found their way beneath her robe to explore the warm, silken flesh. The words he murmured against her throat were unintelligible, spoken in a foreign tongue, yet her body seemed to understand them well enough, arching itself to his touch and moving in tune with his. Aroused all too quickly to a pitch of desire she only half understood, she slipped her hands inside his gaping robe to pull him close. His body was lean and muscular, pressing hard against her own. She moved her open palms across his naked back until she found a pattern of narrow ridges just below his shoulder blades . . . the scars of some past adventure. In a surge of tenderness she pulled him closer still . . .

Suddenly he jerked away from her and raised himself to a sitting position, burying his head in his hands with a groan. Thinking he must be ill, Giulia propped herself on one elbow to look at him, but then she saw he was fighting for self-control and was filled with compassion. 'Oh, my dear,' she said. 'You need not be afraid of hurting me. I'm not made of glass. I want only to . . .'

'Oh, I know well enough what you *want*, madam!' He lifted his head to look at her with savage contempt, taking in her flushed, abandoned appearance, the golden hair tumbling about her naked shoulders, her lips bruised and swollen by his kisses. 'You want me to believe you're Caterina. Yet you give yourself away by behaving like a whore!'

Giulia felt as if her heart had stopped beating. Helplessly she stammered, 'I—I don't understand . . .'

'Do you take me for a fool?' His eyes were almost black with anger. 'Oh, you *look* like Caterina— very alike. 'Tis these that betray you . . .' Roughly he seized her hands and turned them over to stare down at the rough and work-reddened palms. 'As I suspected, you're the maid-servant!'

CHAPTER FOUR

GIULIA SNATCHED her hand from his grasp and pulled up the sheet to cover her near-naked body. 'You're mistaken, my lord,' she protested, her mind seeking desperately for a way out. 'Of course I'm Caterina. How can you . . . ?'

'Don't lie to me, girl! Oh, for a while you almost had me convinced with that show of maidenly reserve. But no woman can hope to deceive a man as to her true nature when she makes love to him.'

Giulia flushed, recalling vividly the shameless way her body had responded to his caresses.

'I should have known something was wrong when I kissed you in the church,' Pietro went on grimly. 'Caterina was stiff and unresponsive in my arms, whereas you, my dear . . .' He left the words unsaid, his gaze resting on her parted lips.

The scar on his cheek was livid against his dark skin. Giulia shrank fearfully back against the pillows.

'Indeed, you've given yourself away again and again by the way you speak and behave, in a manner quite unlike Caterina's, but I put aside my suspicions because I wanted you.' His voice shook with self-disgust. 'Until you touched me with those servant's hands! 'Twas then I came to my senses.'

He rose abruptly and began to pace the room. Giulia stared at him, cursing herself for agreeing to fall in with Ercole Tebaldi's plan. Her father had been so intent on his trade agreement that he had refused to believe anything could go wrong. Now she realised that the whole idea had been doomed from the start. If only she had not listened to him . . . !

'What first gave me the clue as to your true identity was when you called Kasim by name as he helped you from the gondola,' Pietro continued remorselessly. 'I doubt very much if the real Caterina ever set eyes on him. Then I remembered seeing you on the steps when we arrived . . . and again at dinner, when I was struck by your likeness to Caterina. I take it you must be some by-blow of Tebaldi's?'

The harsh words made her wince. She lowered her lashes to hide the pain that must surely show in her eyes.

'And presumably he's a party to this deception, since you cannot have hoped to fool him as well? And Monna Lucia must have known of it—which is no doubt why she refused to attend the wedding.'

He was far more astute, Giulia realised, than any of them had given him credit for.

'But what I *don't* understand,' he persisted, 'is why? Did Caterina so hate the idea of marrying me that she persuaded you to take her place?'

Giulia raised unhappy eyes to his. 'It—it was not quite as you think, my lord.'

He came to stand at the end of the bed, gazing down at her. His anger seemed to have moderated for the moment, perhaps overcome by a genuine curiosity. 'Tell me,' he said in a voice that was quiet yet compelling.

Reluctant though she was to betray her father, Giulia recognised that Pietro Gabrieli would be satisfied with nothing less than the truth. Haltingly, in a small breathless voice, she told him of Caterina's love for Bernardo and of the discovery that had put the wedding plans in jeopardy.

He listened in silence, his lean face betraying no emotion, until she came to their arrival in Venice. Then he interrupted her, saying sharply, 'To the Convent of S. Cecilia? You mean she's with the Sisters of Mercy?'

Giulia bit her lip, wondering if she had said too much. What if he should go to the convent, demanding to see Caterina? Nervously she said, 'Why, yes, but I don't think . . .'

' 'Tis merely that I happen to know the Prioress. Caterina will be in good hands. Mother Maria Innocenti is a remarkable woman, of considerable insight. Indeed, there are many important men in the Republic who turn to her for advice.'

Giulia nodded. 'It was she who told me . . .' She stopped, but when he raised a questioning eyebrow felt obliged to go on. 'She told me it wasn't necessarily a sin for me to take Caterina's place, provided I meant to play my part honestly.' Her voice tailed away at the irony in his eyes.

'And what exactly do you mean by "honestly"?' he queried.

'Only that I—I would try to be a good wife to you . . . and a mother to Gentile.' How feeble that sounded, said aloud. She blushed and looked away rather than encounter the scorn in his eyes.

After a pause he said, 'I don't even know your name.'

' 'Tis Giulia, my lord.'

'*Giulia?*' Comprehension dawned in his eyes. 'In church you gave your name as Caterina Giulia Tebaldi . . . It surprised me at the time, since the name Giulia did not appear on the marriage contract.' Suddenly agitated, he began to pace the room again. 'So we are legally wed?'

'That was my father's intention, sir.'

'The devil it was!' He wheeled round, staring at her so fiercely that she clutched the sheet even tighter than before. 'Who was your mother—or do you not even know?'

'I know she came from Venice. I was raised in the foundling hospital.'

'You mean she was a whore?'

Giulia lifted her chin. 'My father told me she was a woman of character . . . and that he loved her.'

'Aye, for a single night!' he said contemptuously. 'Well, I don't intend to make the same mistake—though you have, I fancy, inherited from her certain talents . . .' His gaze dwelt on the lovely form outlined beneath the thin sheet. 'Indeed, they were almost my undoing.'

At his words, tears sprang unbidden to Giulia's eyes and her throat tightened, preventing her from speaking in her own defence.

His eyes narrowed. 'Are you a virgin?'

'Yes, my lord.'

'I find that very difficult to believe. A maidservant with such undoubted attractions—You must have been besieged by every man for miles around?'

She said angrily, 'It makes no difference whether you believe it or not. I speak the truth.'

'I hope so, for it may shortly be put to the test if we're to have this marriage annulled.'

'Annulled?' Giulia turned pale. 'But how?'

'You can safely leave the details to me. One thing you may be sure of, it shall be arranged with as little loss of dignity as I can manage. I don't intend to make a laughing-stock of myself or of my family.'

And what of me? Giulia thought bitterly.

As if he had read her thoughts, he added, 'Oh, you'll not be sent away empty-handed—provided you do as I say. For the time being you must try to behave as if you were truly Caterina. You're not to confide in anyone, least of all my sister Francesca, who's an inveterate gossip. If you *do* . . . Well, I shall only remind you that murder is the commonest crime in Venice. Bodies are found floating in the canals every day of the week and most are never identified. Do you understand me?'

Giulia nodded, fascinated by the menacing glitter in his eyes. For the first time she saw Pietro Gabrieli as he must appear to his enemies in battle, a ruthless foe who would give no mercy.

'And don't imagine you can hope to deceive me a second time.' He turned to the door. 'Remember, Venice is a city of spies.'

Giulia found her voice. 'Where are you going, my lord?'

'To join the revellers outside.' He smiled mockingly. 'And if they chide me for deserting my bride on her wedding night, I shall tell them you are tired and begged to be left alone. Later, that will no doubt be remembered, and may prove useful evidence.' His eye fell on the table beside the bed, and he strode across to snatch up the plain gold ring he had placed there earlier. Slipping it on to the little finger of his right hand, he held it up before her face. '*This* you will not be wearing tomorrow—or indeed ever!'

Hot tears stung behind Giulia's eyelids, but she blinked them away.

As he turned to the door a second time, he fired a parting shot. 'And if you should think of leaving this room for some reason, let me warn you that Kasim will be outside. From now on he will go with you everywhere, as your personal bodyguard.'

Before she could say another word, he had gone, closing the door behind him. She heard his voice giving orders, and the sound of heavy footsteps. In her imagination she saw the Turk take up his stance outside, legs firmly planted and arms akimbo. She was a prisoner—as much a prisoner as Caterina behind the high stone walls of the convent, both of them trapped by their own foolishness.

For Caterina had undoubtedly been a willing enough party to her own seduction, loving Bernardo without giving a thought to the consequences. And she, Giulia, had allowed herself to be tempted by the promise of riches, a fine house and beautiful clothes . . .

Yet, if she were truly honest, had it not been more than that? Was she not also a little dazzled by the man himself, by his looks and magnetism? She had not lied when she told the Prioress she would love and obey her husband, for she had been ready to do so with all her heart.

She slid lower beneath the sheets, unable to take pleasure in the sensuous feel of silk against her skin or the perfume still lingering from the oils Zoe had rubbed into her body. For she was alone in the huge luxurious bed, rejected by the man who was her husband, who scorned her as unworthy to bear his name. Outside her window she could hear the crack of fireworks, the sound of music across the water and the shouts of the revellers. For them, Carnival was just beginning, a time of joy and celebration.

But for her it was already over, even before it had begun.

* * *

She awoke next morning as pale and heavy-eyed as any bride might be expected to look after her wedding night. There came a gentle knock at the door and Zoe entered with eyes discreetly lowered.

Giulia submitted to her ministrations, finding it restful to be waited on by someone who never spoke and who moved quietly about the room with only the faint jingle of beads to mark her presence. But it seemed odd to sit while Zoe brushed her hair, as she had once brushed Caterina's. She looked at the servant-girl's reflection in the glass. Everything visible—the dark eyes above the veil, the slender hands and feet—suggested a delicate, subtle beauty as mysterious as the land she came from.

'Zoe,' she said impulsively. 'Will you show me your face?'

The girl's eyes widened in shock, followed by something close to panic. She shook her head violently and backed away, pretending to occupy herself at the dower-chest. A little surprised by her vehemence, Giulia wondered if she had unwittingly offended against some law of the harem; she shrugged the matter aside and gave her attention instead to the clothes Zoe was holding up for her inspection.

She chose one of Caterina's most becoming gowns, of blue velvet with a low square neckline. A fillet of gold entwined her hair, which fell in loose curls to her shoulders. The mirror told her she had never looked lovelier. What a difference fine clothes can make even to a serving-maid! she thought ironically.

But as she smoothed down the folds of her skirt she felt the roughness of her hands and looked at them with disgust. Last night they had betrayed her to Pietro, and would surely betray her again to anyone sharp-eyed enough to notice. Resolving to use a lemon paste on them until the skin was white and supple, she pulled on a pair of gloves. These would disguise them for the time being—and would moreover conceal the fact she was not wearing Pietro's ring of approval.

She had forgotten about Kasim until she opened the door. He stood towering over her, waiting for her command.

Giulia hesitated. *Try to behave as if you were truly Caterina*, Pietro had instructed her. No, that would be too difficult, she decided rebelliously. Instead she would continue to play her part as she had begun yesterday.

'I wish to visit Gentile,' she informed Kasim.

He bowed his head and gestured for her to follow. She did so with head held high, determined not to betray the apprehension she felt at the prospect of confronting again the formidable Clarissa Benetti.

Kasim stopped outside a door she recognised. 'Thank you,' she said, and knocked a little tentatively. When there came no reply, her courage almost faltered, but aware of the Turk's watchful eye she opened the door and entered the room.

It was obvious that her arrival was untimely. Monna Clarissa rose to her feet, looking annoyed at the intrusion. Gentile did not even glance up, his entire attention focused on a third person, who was sitting with his back to the door. Giulia could see only the sleeve of a red robe resting along the arm of the chair and a thin, long-fingered hand wearing an onyx ring.

'I'm sorry,' she said hastily. 'I knocked, but nobody answered. I—I wanted only to see Gentile again.'

Monna Clarissa let out a long hissing sigh. '"Tis her—the new wife,' she said, addressing the unseen third person. 'I told you, she came last evening.'

'Ah, yes . . .' A tall man rose from the chair, wearing the scarlet-caped robes of a cardinal. His face was lean as a skull, with a short black beard and eyes set so deep it was impossible to read their expression. When he spoke, his voice was quiet and yet so beautifully modulated that every syllable sounded clear and distinct. ''Tis an honour to make your acquaintance, madonna. I am Lorenzo Benetti, Gentile's uncle.' He held out his hand.

Giulia knelt to kiss his ring. 'My lord.'

He raised her. 'How kind of you to take such an interest in my nephew.'

'Naturally I'm interested. Indeed, I hope that in time he and I shall become great friends.' She smiled at Gentile, but saw that he was still staring at his uncle as if mesmerised. And indeed there *was* something strangely compelling about the Cardinal's sunken eyes and quiet, deliberate voice.

The Cardinal said gravely, 'I'm glad, for Gentile is sorely in need of friends. This house is not a happy place for a child.'

Beneath the gentleness Giulia heard a note of inflexibility. 'I realise his father's absence over the past few years must have affected him deeply,' she said. 'But surely, now that Messer Gabrieli has returned, the situation will improve?'

The Cardinal sighed. 'On the contrary, I fear 'tis since Pietro Gabrieli's return that matters have worsened to their present deplorable state. Regrettably he seems to have turned his back on all Christian values to embrace wholeheartedly the way of the infidel, surrounding himself with thieves and cut-throats.'

Giulia saw that Gentile's eyes had grown enormous. No wonder he's afraid of his father, she thought, if he hears nothing but tales of blood and thunder from his uncle and great-aunt. She said coolly, 'Surely you exaggerate, my lord?'

'I tell you, madonna, this is no fit place to bring up a child. Indeed, if it were not for my aunt, I dread to think what would have become of him.' He bestowed an approving smile on Monna Clarissa, who turned pink with gratification. 'She's acted most unselfishly, offering to live here as companion to Gentile so that the poor child may at least be educated as befits his birth and station.'

Giulia suppressed a pang of irritation. ''Tis far too early for me to make judgments as to the nature of this household,' she said firmly. 'However, you may be assured I'll do my best to see that from now on it *is* a fit place to bring up a child.'

The Cardinal regarded her sadly, almost pityingly. 'I can tell from your face, madonna, that you have an honest, kindly disposition. 'Tis to be hoped you're also resolute, for you'll need moral strength of the highest order if you hope to withstand the corruption that exists in the Ca' Gabrieli.'

Giulia saw the gleam of fanaticism in his hooded eyes and realised that nothing she said or did could possibly allay his deep mistrust of Pietro Gabrieli. She dropped a curtsy. 'My lord, I've trespassed long enough on your time. Please excuse me. I'll come again to see Gentile when it's more convenient.'

As she closed the door behind her she was struck by the irony of the situation. She had just assured the Cardinal in all sincerity that she intended to bring about changes in the Gabrieli household—when in fact her husband was planning an immediate annulment of their marriage! She smiled wryly.

'You look happy, Sister-in-law!' Alessandro must have been waiting outside the door, for he spoke from close beside her, making her jump. 'Did you find Monna Clarissa in a friendlier mood?'

'Not exactly,' Giulia admitted. 'I fear I called at an unfortunate moment. The Cardinal was there.'

'Ah, I should have warned you! His Eminence comes nearly every day at about this time.' Alessandro grinned. He was looking particularly dashing this morning in a yellow tunic with striped hose that showed off his muscular legs. 'And did he warn you how evil we all are, and what a den of iniquity you have fallen into?'

Giulia smiled back, thankful to see a friendly face. 'As a matter of fact, he did!'

'Alas, 'tis all too true!' Alessandro shook his head in mock regret. 'But how lovely you look today, Caterina. I don't know how Pietro could bear to treat you in such a shameful fashion.'

Startled, she looked into his face, but the light green eyes held only mild amusement.

'Did he not tell you? He's gone to the Arsenal, to oversee the fitting out of the galley fleet. No doubt it slipped his memory that a husband's duty on his first day of married life is to show his bride over her new establishment. Never mind, I shall perform the task on his behalf.' He tucked his arm through hers and led her towards the stairs. 'Where would you like to start?'

Giulia laughed. 'I leave it entirely to you.'

'Very wise.' He drew her closer to whisper in her ear. 'Tell me, why is Kasim following so close on our heels.'

She became aware that the Turk was padding softly along behind them in his leather slippers. 'Pietro ordered him to accompany me everywhere.'

'Did he indeed?' Alessandro sounded impressed. 'He must value you above pearls, Caterina, if he's given you Kasim as your bodyguard. Normally he doesn't even venture from the house without him.'

It isn't that he values me, she wanted to say, but that he doesn't trust me!

When they reached the ground floor where the kitchens were situated and the house gondolas kept when not in use, Giulia said impulsively, 'Alessandro, I can look over the house at any time. What I should like above all things is to go into the city and see the Carnival.'

He seemed pleased by her suggestion. 'Why not? You're far too beautiful to be burdened by housewifely cares so early in your married life. I'll send for your cloak.' He gave orders to Kasim and then told the boatman, who was catnapping on the steps below them, to make ready the gondola.

Giulia's spirits rose. She was beginning to find the atmosphere of the Ca' Gabrieli oppressive and longed to escape, if only for an hour or so.

When Kasim returned with her mantle, Alessandro took it from him and swung it round her shoulders. He helped her into the gondola, but when Kasim made as if to come with him he waved him away. 'You can safely leave Monna Caterina in my hands. I'll see she comes to no harm.'

As they slid away from the steps and through the water-gate, Giulia caught sight of Kasim's frustrated expression. 'Oh dear,' she murmured. 'I hope he won't be in trouble with Pietro.'

'Most certainly he will, but Kasim is used to trouble,' Alessandro said unconcernedly. He started to pull the curtains around the little cabin.

'Please . . . leave them open,' Giulia begged.

'Today I want to see Venice in all her glory.'

'And let Venice see *you*?' He gave her an amused look. 'What an innocent creature you are, Caterina! You come as a breath of fresh air straight from Verona, where life must be so much less complicated.'

'What do you mean?' she asked, disconcerted. 'Isn't it acceptable for a married woman to go out in Venice, even with an escort?'

'*Especially* with an escort!' His eyes laughed at her. 'But fortunately this is Carnival time, when anything is acceptable. Though I think perhaps we'd be wise to buy you a mask at the earliest opportunity.'

They disembarked at St Mark's Square. Today Giulia was able to take more notice of her surroundings and saw as if for the first time the lacy pink colonnades of the ducal palace and the twin columns supporting the Lion of St Mark's and the figure of St Theodore. Even higher, atop the tall campanile, perched a gilded angel, lifting her wings to the sun.

The Piazzetta was crowded, citizens of Venice jostling for elbow-room amidst the mass of sailors and traders from other lands. Most of the better-dressed women were masked, Giulia noticed as she watched them tottering along on their high *choppines* which elevated them above the flooded pavements so commonplace in Venice. Indeed, so many curious glances were cast in her direction that she felt much happier when they had purchased a black lace mask that hid the upper part of her face. 'Now you're anonymous,' Alessandro said, fixing it carefully in place. 'You may go where you like and do as you please, without fear of discovery.'

They strolled through the network of narrow

streets leading off the square, stopping to watch the acrobats and jugglers. At one time they entered a quiet alley made dark by a high wall, and as they passed a doorway Giulia saw from the name above that this was the landward entrance to the Convent of S. Cecilia. She shivered involuntarily. When Alessandro asked if she was cold, she said, No, it was merely a ghost walking over her grave.

Aye, Caterina's ghost! she thought as they emerged once more into the sunlit piazza, for it seemed as though her half-sister might as well be dead as shut away behind those forbidding walls.

But so infectious was the spirit of gaiety abroad that in a little while she shook off her depression. She saw that many of the other women were far more richly dressed than herself and ostentatiously bedecked in jewels and gold chains. One woman, wearing a crimson gown and elaborate head-dress studded with pearls, smiled graciously at Alessandro and he in turn bowed low as if to a queen.

'Who was that?' Giulia whispered curiously.

'Laura Rocco,' he replied. 'The most famous courtesan in all Venice, renowned for her brains as well as her beauty.' Giulia looked at him with such amazement that he burst out laughing. 'Did you not realise that nearly every woman you see is a courtesan? Venice is a sea-port, full of sailors. You'll find more harlots here than in any other city in Europe.'

Giulia was silent, occupied with her thoughts. So Laura Rocco was a 'woman of Venice', like her own mother. For the first time it occurred to her to wonder if her mother were still alive. She had somehow assumed from the way Ercole had spoken that she was long since dead, but in fact he had said nothing to confirm that assumption. What if her mother *were* alive . . . and still walking the streets of Venice?

'I've shocked you,' Alessandro said, watching her face. 'I'm sorry. I was forgetting you'd led such a sheltered life.'

'I'm not shocked,' she assured him quickly. 'I was only wondering what sort of age is Laura Rocco? She cannot be young . . .'

He shrugged. 'In her thirties, perhaps. But she's very well preserved. And no wonder, with so many wealthy protectors to cushion her existence!'

Giulia gazed after the beautiful courtesan, who was still making her stately way across the square. She felt an overwhelming urge to run after her, to ask if she had ever borne a child . . .

But how ridiculous! she told herself sternly. That would be too much of a coincidence, especially when one remembered how many courtesans there were in Venice.

She was so quiet on the journey home that Alessandro inquired if something was wrong. She took off her mask to rub her eyes, and said without thinking, ' 'Tis only that I'm tired. I hardly slept last night . . .' As soon as she saw the teasing look in Alessandro's eyes, she realised what she had said, and coloured hotly.

'Pietro also looked a little pale when he left for the Arsenal this morning,' he commented. 'I can't imagine why!'

She did not even attempt to answer, but as the gondola carried them back to the Ca' Gabrieli she reflected with some surprise that Alessandro could not have been among the revellers last night or he would have known her husband had not stayed with her.

. . . Unless Pietro had not after all carried out his threat to make public the fact their marriage was unconsummated? She was glad of the gloves that hid her hands from Alessandro's curious eyes, so that he could not see the ring of approval was missing.

Pietro was awaiting their return, pacing up and down the length of the portego. When they appeared, he swung round to glare at them, unsmiling.

'Ah, there you are, Brother!' Alessandro said pleasantly. 'Have you had a satisfactory morning? I trust there'll be no delay in your sailing?'

A muscle twitched in Pietro's jaw. Ignoring his brother, he addressed himself to Giulia. 'Where have you been?'

Although her heart had begun to pound at the sight of his grim expression, she managed to speak calmly. 'Alessandro has been very kind. He offered to show me over the house, but I told him I'd prefer to go out.'

'Without Kasim,' Pietro snapped. 'When I expressly gave orders he was to go with you everywhere.'

'We had no need of him,' Alessandro said in a careless tone. 'I assure you, Brother, I'm perfectly well able to take care of Caterina.'

'That's not the point!' Pietro glared at him. 'I *will* not have my orders disobeyed.'

Giulia sensed the hostility crackling between the two brothers. She said quickly, 'Please—it was nobody's fault but mine. You must not blame Alessandro . . . or Kasim.'

Her husband turned to seize her wrist, startling her by the speed of his action. 'Come with me. I want to speak with you alone.' He half-pulled her towards the stairs.

Behind them Alessandro gave a low laugh. 'Such impatience!' he said mockingly. 'Not that I blame you, Brother. Not that I blame you in the least!'

CHAPTER FIVE

NOT UNTIL he had thrust her into the bedchamber and closed the door behind them did Pietro release her wrist. He stood glowering at her, his dark brows drawn together. 'So this is how you intend to keep your word?' he said accusingly. 'By disobeying my orders as soon as my back is turned!'

Giulia faced him with defiance, rubbing her bruised wrist. 'My lord, I promised only to behave as if I were Caterina . . .'

'And do you think Caterina would have ventured into the city on the first day of her marriage, with my brother as escort?' He gave a short, humourless laugh. 'The idea wouldn't even enter her head!'

Recognising there was some truth in this, Giulia murmured, 'No one has seen my face. I wore a mask.'

'A *mask*?' His gaze slid contemptuously over the close-fitting bodice of her blue velvet gown, following the curve of her bosom above the slim waist. 'Ay, like every other whore abroad at Carnival time!'

Giulia winced. 'I wish you would not call me by that name, my lord. 'Tis quite unjustified, I assure you.'

'You forget, my dear, that I've evidence to the contrary.' Menacingly he took a step towards her, looking down into her troubled face. 'I'm warning you, keep away from Alessandro! He's not to be trusted.'

'But he's your own brother! Surely you don't count Alessandro among your enemies?'

Pietro's eyes gleamed. 'I count every man my enemy—until he proves otherwise.'

She found his nearness overwhelming. Feigning a calm she did not feel, she moved away from him, saying lightly, 'I'm afraid you've been at war too long, my lord. You see treachery everywhere, even in your own home.'

'With good reason, I assure you!' Following her, he seized her arm and swung her round to face him again. 'How can I make you understand? Alessandro devotes his entire life to the pursuit of women—and believe me, there's no woman he'd rather pursue than his brother's wife, whoever she might be. To make a cuckold of me would give him the keenest personal pleasure. Moreover he wouldn't hesitate to use his power over you to gain his own ends.'

Giulia stared up at him, trying to fathom what lay behind his anger. Was he—could he be *jealous* of Alessandro? A spark of hope was born in her heart, only to be doused by his next words.

'Nor do I wish you to see my son again.'

'Gentile? But why ever not?'

'Are you so insensitive? Don't you realise the harm you could do?'

That he should accuse *her* of being insensitive! Angrily she pulled away from his grasp. 'What possible harm can there be in my visiting Gentile?' she demanded. 'The poor child sees no one but his uncle and that—that sour-faced old harridan of a great-aunt! He's made to spend all day at his studies, bent over a desk. 'Tis a most unnatural existence for a boy of his age.'

Pietro seemed unmoved by her outburst. 'I agree his life so far hasn't been a particularly happy one. However, now that I'm home . . .'

'Home—for how long?' she said scornfully. 'At any moment you'll be sailing for the Levant—and Gentile will be left once more in the care of the Benettis. Don't you realise they're turning him against you? He hears nothing but stories of your cruelty, your—your sinful way of life. No wonder he's afraid of you!'

He said nothing. Only a small nerve pulsing in his temple betrayed his annoyance.

Giulia was carried away on a tide of indignation. 'Oh, I'm not saying I could wean him away from the influence of the Benettis, but at least while I'm here I could teach him some games or tell him stories . . .' Her voice tailed off as she caught sight of his face. She concluded lamely, 'Surely there could be no harm in that? I'm thinking only of Gentile.'

'I'm thinking of Gentile too.' His tone was ice-cold. 'If you go on seeing the child he may become too attached to you. To let him grow fond of someone he must inevitably lose again would be a far greater cruelty than anything the Benettis have yet accused me of.' His eyes narrowed. 'Or was that your intention—to make the child dependent on you and thus use him as a weapon? Perhaps you were hoping to persuade me against the annulment of our marriage?'

Giulia kept her temper with difficulty. 'I wouldn't dream of trying to persuade you against the annulment, my lord. 'Tis plain your mind's made up.'

'Ay, so it is—and I've today sent word to your father informing him of my intent.' He added cynically, 'No doubt he'll soon be returning hot-foot to Venice, anxious to protect his interests.'

Giulia's gaze faltered. 'The trade agreement—you wouldn't seek to cancel it?'

'Why not?' He glared at her. 'Ercole Tebaldi has cheated me at every turn. Why should I honour my agreement with a man who's already proved himself nothing but a dishonest rogue?'

'You mistake his motives, my lord. He sought only to protect his family . . .'

'You show him more loyalty than he deserves.' He gave her an odd look, half-pitying, half-contemptuous. 'Tell me truthfully, Giulia—do you love your father?'

It was the first time he had called her by her own name. Caught off guard, she stammered, 'I—I'm grateful to him.'

'For what?'

'Why, for bringing me up in his own home . . .'

'As a servant!' His voice was sharp with scorn. 'When first I saw you, you were barefoot in the farmyard with an apronful of eggs while your half-sister lay languishing abed in silken sheets. And for this you're *grateful*?'

Giulia flushed. 'He could have left me in the foundling hospital.'

'Yes, so he could! But no doubt it suited him better to have you under his own roof, as unpaid maid-servant to Caterina.'

'My lord, you're too ready to believe the worst of people! My father may be a little foolish on occasions, but he's always been kind.'

'Was he being *kind* when he forced you to take your sister's place?'

'He didn't force me! I—I did so of my own free will.'

'But you must have known such an ill-conceived scheme was bound to fail?'

'I knew there were risks,' she admitted. 'But I was prepared to take them.'

'I suppose you saw this marriage as a means of escape.' His voice was ironic, yet held a note of grudging admiration. 'One can hardly blame you for gambling on the consequences.'

She raised her head proudly to meet his eyes—and surprised there an expression that made her catch her breath.

'Oh, your father knew well enough what he was doing when he offered you as a substitute,' Pietro said softly. 'He knew that even if I discovered the deception you would present a considerable temptation . . .' A flame leapt in his eyes. As if to hide it, he turned away sharply and went to stare out of the window. When he spoke again it was in a strangely altered tone. 'Unfortunately for both of you, I'm not so easily seduced.'

Giulia stared at his implacable back, not daring to speak. She would get nowhere by opposing him, she saw that clearly. To win his trust she must employ more subtle means . . .

He turned to face her. 'I shall strike a bargain with you, Giulia,' he said levelly. 'If you do as I ask—that is keep away from my brother and my son as long as you remain in this house—then I will tell your father when he comes that I've decided to honour our trade agreement.'

She gazed at him, uncertain how to respond.

'This means, of course,' he continued, 'that you must stay in your own apartment and not set foot in the rest of my house. Nor must you go out into the city.'

The colour left her cheeks. 'You would keep me a prisoner?'

'I have no choice.' When she said nothing, he prompted impatiently, 'Well?—Do you agree?'

For Ercole's sake, how could she refuse? 'Why, yes. But won't people think it a little odd?'

'You may leave that to me. I'll think of some explanation.' He clapped his hands loudly and Zoe appeared. With a fluttering of draperies and a jangle of beads she came to stand submissively before him. He spoke to her in Turkish, in so kindly a voice that Giulia stared at him in surprise. But then she saw Zoe's dark eyes luminous with love and devotion for her master, and her heart missed a beat. Ay, she thought despairingly, that's the only kind of woman he understands—one who will abase herself before him and offer an unquestioning, slavish adoration. To such a woman he could show kindness and even love . . . but not to a woman with a mind of her own who would meet him on equal terms.

As if to prove her point, Pietro's expression hardened when he turned back to address her. 'I've told Zoe she's to take away the clothes you brought with you so that you may not be tempted to disobey my orders a second time.'

Giulia tried to conceal her dismay. 'Do you not trust me, my lord?'

'Experience has taught me to trust no one. Unlike you and your father I'm not by nature a gambler. I've learned never to take chances.'

'And what am I expected to wear?' she inquired a little tartly. 'Surely you would not have me go naked?'

His gaze flickered, as if uncertain whether or not

she was being deliberately provocative. 'You'll be provided with a suitable alternative,' he said stiffly. 'And I warn you, there's no point in your trying to leave this room. Kasim will be instructed to use force if necessary to prevent you.'

'Heavens,' she said, keeping her tone light. 'No one would believe I had actually *agreed* to strike a bargain with you. How would you have behaved, I wonder, if I'd *refused* to do as you asked?'

He said dryly, 'Most like I should have taken the same precautions. The only difference lies in the outcome. I would remind you, Giulia, 'tis your father who stands to lose if you disobey.'

She lowered her lashes to veil the resentment in her eyes. Pray heaven Ercole Tebaldi returns quickly to Venice, she thought, to put matters right between himself and the man he had attempted to deceive. Until that time she must learn to guard her tongue.

She said meekly, 'I've no intention of disobeying you, my lord.'

For an instant he seemed about to say something more, then changed his mind and left the room, closing the door behind him.

All the anger and frustration Giulia had so far managed to suppress rose up into her throat, almost choking her. A prisoner . . . forbidden to go where she pleased or speak to whom she chose! How could any man be so autocratic . . . so ruthlessly tyrannical? Enraged, she swung round and would have flung herself screaming on the bed had she not suddenly caught sight of Zoe hovering behind her. So self-effacing was the servant-girl that Giulia had quite forgotten her existence, but now she saw Zoe's frightened eyes fixed on her face and realised the poor girl was terrified that she would refuse to comply with Pietro's orders.

With a supreme effort Giulia regained her self-control. 'Come,' she said, turning her back so that Zoe might undo the tiny buttons fastening the bodice of her gown. 'Do as your master bids you.'

The girl's fingers were trembling so much they made her clumsy, but Giulia stood patiently until the blue velvet gown descended to the floor, followed by her undergarments. With a sigh she stepped out of them, saying, 'For pity's sake bring me something to cover myself. I care not what it may be.'

Zoe gathered up the pile of clothing and disappeared from the room. She returned almost at once with a loose-fitting robe of green silk edged with gold and slipped it over Giulia's head.

Now my transformation is complete, Giulia thought as she stared down at the flowing, alien garment. I am a woman of the seraglio: neither wife nor chosen concubine, merely a slave to be chastened and cowed into submission.

She climbed the dais to the divan and sank back against the cushions, trying to shut her ears to the tantalising sounds of the city outside her window. Dimly she was aware when Zoe came back into the room to light the lamps, and later still a meal was set beside her on a table. She had little appetite and ate only a few morsels of bread and goat-cheese. But she drank all the wine, draining the goblet to the last drop, and soon fell into a deep, dreamless sleep.

After some time she awoke with an aching head and a parched throat. Her limbs felt languorous and heavy as lead. She called for Zoe to prepare a bath, hoping it might restore her senses, and emerged from the water feeling a little refreshed.

She allowed Zoe to clothe her in the silken shift she had worn on her wedding night and called for more wine to slake her thirst. No sooner did she lie down upon the bed than she fell asleep again.

Hours passed. Perhaps days. She lost all count of time. There was nothing for her to do but eat and sleep. She took frequent baths to relieve the monotony and encouraged Zoe to brush her hair for long periods at a time, finding the measured strokes soothing to her perpetual headache. But the maidservant was an unsatisfactory companion, always so silent and subservient. If only she could *talk* to someone! Enforced solitude was a cruel punishment for someone of her lively, gregarious disposition. Sometimes she wondered if she were going mad.

For she became convinced she was being watched. Often she would awake with a start, thinking she heard someone moving about in the room; and once when she was bathing she saw a movement in the curtains over the door. Yet, when she had gone to look, there was no one there.

One night she stirred to see a shadowy figure standing beside her bed, holding aloft a candle. Involuntarily she lifted her hand towards him in a helpless, imploring gesture, but the silent visitor made no response. At last her hand fell limply to her side and she closed her eyes, overcome once more by sleep. In the morning when she awoke she told herself it must have been a dream. Or perhaps Kasim, come to check she was safely in her bed.

But not Pietro. He had not come near her.

When at last he did come to see her he caught her unawares, still in her nightshift though it was almost noon, and dozing fitfully on the divan with her unbound hair spread over the cushions. As he stood looking down at her, there lurked in the back of his eyes something oddly akin to pity.

Giulia struggled to sit up. 'My lord, I—I thought you must have sailed . . .'

'Not yet.'

'I—I don't even know what day it is.' She rubbed her aching eyes. 'How long have I been here?'

'Five days.'

'Five days!' She was shocked. 'But what of my father? Has he not returned to Venice?'

'No. Nor has there been any word of him.' Pietro's face was inscrutable. 'It seems as though he's not nearly so concerned about our trade agreement as you thought.'

'But I don't understand . . .' She shook her head, trying to clear the fog from her brain. 'Something must have happened to him.'

'I doubt it,' Pietro said dryly. 'More likely he's lying low, hoping I'll be so busy preparing for my voyage that I shall forget how he tried to trick me.'

Giulia realised this was probably true. It would be typical of Ercole to behave like an ostrich, convinced that if he took no action everything would turn out for the best.

Pietro continued, 'Or he may be hoping that by now I shall have grown so enamoured of your beauty that I've decided to accept the substitution after all.'

Something in his tone made her aware that the flimsy nightshift revealed every curve of her body. She flushed. 'My lord, how long do you mean to keep me imprisoned in this manner?'

'You must be patient. The time will soon pass.'

Tears stung behind her eyelids. 'How can you say that? You don't know what it's like?'

'Oh, I know well enough.' He bent closer, his eyes suddenly fierce. 'Once I too was held prisoner—in a bare cell infested by rats, with nothing to eat and drink but bread and water. You, my dear, are being treated with the utmost consideration—far more, indeed, then you deserve!'

She shrank back against the cushions, startled by the suppressed violence in his voice. Yet once again she saw the bright flame of desire leap in his eyes and knew that at least part of his resentment was directed not against her but against himself. He wanted her . . . and despised himself for his weakness. She stared up at him, fascinated by the lean dark face so close to hers, his mouth hovering only inches from her own. Her lips parted in anticipation.

But he straightened and clapped his hands. When Zoe appeared, he ordered her to bring more wine for her mistress.

Giulia felt weak with disappointment. 'I—I don't want . . .'

He waved aside her protests. ''Tis good for you. It will make you sleep.'

'I sleep too much already . . .'

Ignoring the plaintive note in her voice, he turned on his heel and left the room.

An unpleasant suspicion awoke in Giulia's mind. When Zoe brought the wine, she refused to drink it, even though her throat was parched and rough. The servant-girl grew agitated, but Giulia remained firm. 'Bring me fruit,' she commanded, and from that moment on she quenched her thirst only with the juice of grapes and oranges.

* * *

Almost at once she began to feel better. Her head cleared and her limbs lost their languid heaviness. But as soon as she returned to normal she understood why Pietro had given orders for her wine to be drugged, for she was seized by a terrible restlessness. The hours dragged by interminably. Now that her brain was active again she longed for something to occupy it.

Her body too demanded to be exercised. She took to pacing up and down the room, from the window to the door, from the bed to the divan, while Zoe looked on anxiously.

It was while she was thus engaged that she heard a woman's voice outside her door, furiously declaiming, 'Stand aside this instant! I *insist* upon seeing my sister-in-law.'

Giulia could well imagine the scene outside—the small but forceful figure of Francesca confronting the rock-like Kasim—and wondered who would win.

The question was answered when the door burst open and Francesca marched determinedly into the room. 'My dear Caterina . . .' She stopped short when she saw Giulia's pale face, the loose eastern robe of green silk. 'So 'tis true—you *are* unwell! But what is the matter?'

Giulia opened her mouth to reply and then stopped, her eyes going to the huge figure of Kasim lurking in the doorway.

Francesca muttered something beneath her breath and closed the door firmly in the Turk's face. 'Now we're alone. You can tell me honestly—what is amiss?'

Giulia saw she must be on her guard—with Francesca more than anyone, for another woman might be too perceptive. She attempted a smile.

'Why, nothing! I'm perfectly well.'

'You don't *look* well! And Pietro's steward informed me that you wished to see no one.'

'That's true.'

'But *why*?' Francesca peered searchingly into her face. 'There *is* something wrong, I can tell! Are matters not as they should be between you and Pietro?'

Giulia blushed and looked down at her hands. Too late she realised they were ungloved, and made a hasty attempt to hide them within the folds of her gown.

But Francesca's eyes were too sharp. She gave a start of dismay. 'Oh, my dear—he hasn't given you the ring! So *that*'s why you're afraid to be seen in public?'

'I'd rather not talk about it, if you don't mind.'

'Nonsense! You must tell me everything. Did I not promise your father I would give you all the help and advice I could?' Francesca gave her a reassuring smile. 'Your plight is not so unusual as you may think, my dear. Many young brides are alarmed at first by the demands their husbands make upon them. 'Tis nothing to be ashamed of.'

In a blinding flash of clarity Giulia saw how cleverly Pietro had prepared the way for the annulment of their marriage. By claiming she was unwell and wished to keep to her room he had already sown the seeds of suspicion that the bride was unwilling . . . while the bridegroom on the other hand was displaying the utmost forbearance! For a moment she was tempted to tell Francesca the truth—that on the contrary it was Pietro and not she who refused to consummate their marriage.

But of course Francesca would not believe her . . .

She bit her lip. ' 'Tis not quite as you think.'

'My dear Caterina, I'm a married woman and shall not be shocked at anything you say. I know all too well how inconsiderate men can be . . . and I fear Pietro's sensibilities may have become blunted by his years at war.' She perched herself on the divan. 'Now, put aside your modesty and tell me plainly—has he tried to force you against your will?'

'No! 'Tis nothing like that, I assure you.'

'I'm relieved to hear it. Tiresome though he may be, Pietro is still my favourite brother and I wouldn't like to think him capable of such infamous conduct.' She patted the divan invitingly. 'Why don't you sit down? For, I warn you, I don't intend to leave this room until you've told me the truth.'

Unwillingly Giulia sat, keeping her eyes downcast.

Francesca looked at her with a puzzled expression. 'You know, the first time I saw you, I thought, Thank heaven! This time Pietro has found someone who will be a true wife to him . . . This time it will be different.'

'Different?' Giulia glanced up, her curiosity aroused in spite of herself.

'Oh, my foolish tongue!' Francesca looked repentant, then smiled ruefully and confided, 'You must know that Pietro's first wife was hardly more than a child when he married her . . . and still a child in spirit and behaviour when she died giving birth to Gentile. I think he has never forgiven himself for that. Indeed, I believe 'tis partly why he delayed so long in coming to Verona to claim you as his bride. He was waiting for you to grow up.'

Giulia stared at her, unable to speak.

'But *you* are not a child, Caterina.' Francesca's

tone was gentle but firm. 'No one looking at you could be in any doubt that you're a woman, ripe and ready for love. You can hardly blame Pietro for . . .'

At this point the door flew open to admit a furious Pietro. He took in the scene at a glance and strode towards them, his eyes blazing.

A woman of lesser spirit might have been intimidated. Not so Francesca. She rose to face him defiantly, standing in front of Giulia as if to screen her from his wrath.

'What are *you* doing here?' he demanded rudely. 'My orders are that no one is to enter this room.'

'And I don't take orders from *you*, Brother!' Francesca glared at him. 'I came to see Caterina . . . and to offer my help.'

'She needs no help from you, Francesca . . . or indeed from anyone.'

'How little you understand women!' With a dramatic sweep of her hand Francesca indicated the silent, white-faced Giulia. 'Anyone can see at a glance that the poor girl is unhappy—and no wonder, left alone day after day in this gloomy chamber.'

Pietro looked uncomfortable. 'I'm about to set sail on a lengthy voyage, as well you know. Naturally I must spend time with my ship.'

'Neglecting your bride most shamefully! 'Tis plain you've not the least idea how to treat a gently nurtured girl like Caterina. I'm not surprised she finds your advances repugnant!'

'*Francesca!*' Giulia could bear it no longer. 'I beg you, say no more. Oh, I know you mean well, but you don't understand. This matter concerns only Pietro and myself, no one else.' She went to stand beside him as if to demonstrate their unity. 'The kindest thing you can do is to leave us alone.'

Francesca stared at her disbelievingly. 'Are you serious?'

'You heard what my wife said.' Pietro's tone was sardonic. 'We wish to be left alone.'

Francesca drew her brows together in a perplexed frown. 'Very well,' she said at last. 'If that's what you want.' She turned away, but at the door she hesitated. 'If you should need me, Caterina, you have only to send word . . .'

'I'll see you to your gondola.' Pietro escorted his sister firmly from the room.

He returned to find Giulia still standing where he had left her. 'Before I arrived,' he demanded, 'what did she say to you?'

'She noticed I wasn't wearing your ring,' Giulia said in a flat, unemotional tone. 'Naturally she was curious to know why.'

He reached her in a single stride and jerked her chin towards him so that he might look into her face. 'And what did you tell her?'

'Nothing. I let her draw her own conclusions.' Giulia gave him a straight look, too shaken by her confrontation with Francesca to dissemble further. 'Which were, of course, that our marriage has not been consummated owing to the reluctance of the bride. Well, my lord? Are you not pleased? Isn't that what you wanted?'

He dropped his hand from her chin. 'It had to be done,' he said heavily. 'I had no choice.'

'Perhaps not. But drugging my wine—that was quite unnecessary. You need not have gone to those lengths to ensure my obedience.'

He had the grace to look ashamed. ' 'Twas for your own good. I feared you might find time passing too slowly and grow bored.'

'So you took no chances, as is your custom?' Giulia smiled an ironic little half-smile. 'Well, you're right—I *am* bored. And if I'm to be imprisoned here much longer I would ask for a minor indulgence.'

He was on his guard at once. 'And what might that be?'

'Books, my lord.' She saw his incomprehension and explained, 'I must have something to occupy my mind. Surely you cannot object to my reading?'

He stared at her. 'You can *read*?'

'Of course. My father arranged for me to share Caterina's education. Our tutor was a Franciscan friar who came every day to the house.' She did not add that she had been far quicker at her studies than Caterina, who was inclined to be lazy. 'If I might be allowed to visit your library?'

'Ah!' His lip curled in derision. 'So that's your ploy! You would leave this room on the pretext of visiting my library—and no doubt you'd soon find a way of extending that liberty to include the rest of the house.'

Giulia fought down her rising anger. 'Once again, my lord, you see mischief where none is intended. Choose some books for me, if you will, and bring them here. I ask only that they be lively and entertaining, to help relieve the tedium of my present existence.'

Their eyes met and clashed. For a long moment he subjected her to so piercing a scrutiny that Giulia felt he must see into her very soul; but she held her head high, refusing to look away. After all, she had nothing to hide.

At length he said reluctantly, 'Very well. Kasim will take you to my library . . . and wait with you there till you've made your choice.'

Giulia inclined her head in graceful acceptance. 'Thank you, my lord.' But as he turned to the door, she added, 'There is another favour . . .'

He glanced at her sharply. 'Yes?'

'That I may be allowed something to drink that hasn't been tampered with. One cannot always quench one's thirst sufficiently with fruit.'

He gave a brief nod. 'I've already given instructions to that effect. From now on you may safely drink anything that Zoe brings you.'

'Thank you, my lord.'

He hesitated, his gaze lingering on her pale face, the dark smudges beneath her eyes. 'I fear my treatment of you has impaired your looks,' he observed. 'I'm sorry.'

Giulia's heart gave a startled leap.

'But you're still the most desirable woman in Venice, if that's any comfort to you.' His voice was harsh, as if the words were dragged out of him against his will. 'Would to God things were different between us . . .'

Turning swiftly, he strode from the room.

Giulia remained staring after him. Now she was certain that he was by no means indifferent to her, no matter how hard he might try to conceal the fact. Given time, he must surely relent . . .

But time was not on her side. Soon he would be leaving on a voyage that might take him away from home for weeks, even months. She closed her eyes, swaying a little. The thought of losing him now was unbearable. For the first time she knew how Caterina must have felt at the prospect of losing Bernardo. *You've never been in love— You cannot possibly understand how I feel!* As Caterina's accusing words came into her mind, tears welled up from beneath her closed lids and slid unheeding down her cheeks.

For now she understood well enough! At long last she too had fallen in love—but with a strange, unapproachable man who regarded her as someone not to be trusted . . . and who would not allow himself to love her in return.

CHAPTER SIX

THE LIBRARY of the Ca' Gabrieli was an impressive room; its floors of marble, the walls hung with gilded leather. Giulia stood entranced upon the threshold, gazing in wonderment at the shelves upon shelves of books set at right-angles across the room. This must be the work of a great collector—most likely the man whose portrait hung above the mantelshelf, looking sternly down at her.

She turned to Kasim. 'Wait outside,' she ordered. 'I shall be some while. There's so much to choose from.'

He nodded and took up his customary stance facing the corridor. She closed the door on him, breathing a sigh of relief. Alone at last . . . and in civilised surroundings, away from the oppressive atmosphere of the bedchamber.

She advanced into the room, casting her eye at random over the shelves. Virgil, Plutarch, Dante . . . all notable works, but hardly calculated to relieve her boredom. She moved on, the brocade caftan she had donned to cover her filmsy gown making a soft swishing sound as its heavy skirt dragged across the floor. She stopped . . . and heard a small scuffling noise that continued for a second or two longer. Her heart beat faster. Was she being spied on, even here?

She told herself not to be foolish, that too much

solitude had made her fanciful. Suppressing her unease, she tried to concentrate on selecting a book from the bewildering array in front of her.

At last she found what she wanted—two volumes of stories from Boccaccio's *Decameron Nights*. These she had been forbidden to read in Verona. Monna Lucia had pronounced them unsuitable on the grounds of lewdness and had hidden them in her own room for fear they might have a disturbing effect on the minds of young girls. Giulia smiled delightedly. Yes, the tales of Boccaccio would do very well to enliven her captivity! Taking them from the shelf, she turned away, and out of the corner of her eye saw a slight but perceptible movement in the curtains on the other side of the room. Her initial start of fear gave way to indignation.

'Who's there?' she demanded sharply. 'Come out at once, whoever you are . . .'

After a moment's hesitation Gentile appeared, his eyes wide with terror, his small face creased up in readiness for tears.

Giulia was on her knees before him in an instant. 'Gentile, don't cry! I'm not angry. You frightened me, that's all.' She put down the books and took hold of his thin little arms. 'Heavens, I thought you were a ghost!'

He gazed at her uncertainly, his lower lip trembling.

'But why didn't you speak out when you heard me come in?' she asked. 'Is it because you're not supposed to visit the library? Does Monna Clarissa know you're here?'

As she saw the look of panic on his face, Giulia realised she had only alarmed him further and hastened to put right her mistake. 'But of course—

you were hiding from me! How stupid of me not to guess. 'Tis a splendid place to play hide-and-seek, with all these shelves.'

He seemed so uncomprehending that Giulia wondered if he had ever heard of the game—or any other, for that matter. But then she could not imagine Monna Clarissa indulging in so light-hearted a pastime—or indeed his uncle, the formidable Cardinal Benetti.

She rose to her feet. 'Well, now 'tis my turn to hide. Close your eyes.'

He obeyed her at once. It seemed as if obedience were second nature to him. Did he never rebel?

'You must count to ten,' she said. 'Aloud, so that I may know when you're coming to look for me.'

'One, two, three . . .' he began in a low, hoarse whisper. With a sense of shock Giulia realised that was the first time she had ever heard his voice. Dear God, she thought, what kind of tyrannical upbringing can produce a child so lacking in spirit that he is even afraid to speak?

So stunned was she by this discovery that she failed to move until he had reached a count of seven. Hastily she took cover behind the nearest shelf.

'. . . ten,' he concluded.

Giulia waited, holding her breath. Would he show sufficient initiative to come and look for her? She crouched on the floor, pretending to hide her head within the wide sleeves of her caftan. 'Ready!' she called encouragingly.

After what seemed like an age, she felt a light tap on her shoulder. 'I can see you, madonna,' Gentile said in a hoarse voice. 'You are not hidden very well.'

'Oh, oh!' Giulia cried in pretended dismay, and

stood up laughing. To her delight she saw his lips begin to curve into a smile, and then a subdued chuckle escaped him. 'Now it's your turn again,' she said, closing her eyes.

By the time she reached 'ten' she could still hear movement in the room. 'Are you ready?' she called; when there came no reply, she opened her eyes.

A stricken, white-faced Gentile stood before her, and behind him Pietro, his hands resting on his son's shoulders, his dark eyes holding an unspoken accusation.

Giulia's heart faltered. 'My lord!'

Without taking his eyes from her face Pietro pushed his son firmly towards the door. 'Go back to your aunt,' he commanded. 'I've no doubt she's concerned about you.'

Giulia waited until Gentile was safely out of the room before attempting to defend herself. She said quickly, 'He was here when I arrived, hiding behind the curtain. When I discovered him he was so frightened that I pretended it was all a game. I don't believe anyone has ever played with him before. He was just beginning to lose his fear of me when you—you came upon us.' She found the steadiness of his gaze unnerving and began to stammer guiltily. 'I was so intent upon gaining his confidence that I forgot your instructions completely. Indeed, they never entered my head.'

'You have a conveniently short memory,' he observed.

Anger flared within her. 'Well, what else should I have done?' she demanded. 'Would you have me scream and run from the room the instant he stepped from behind the curtain? You're being unreasonable, my lord! I came here to find something to read, not to keep a secret assignation with your six-year-old son!'

He regarded her for a long moment, his expression enigmatic. Then he inquired unexpectedly, 'And *did* you find something to read?'

'Yes, I . . .' Disconcerted, she looked round for the two volumes she had put down on the floor while playing with Gentile. 'Ah, there they are.' She picked them up, tucking them a little furtively beneath her arm.

'Show me.' When she obeyed, somewhat reluctantly, he looked at the titles and smiled. 'The *Decameron Nights* . . . Stories devised to amuse a group of young women during a period of enforced idleness. How very appropriate! I hope you enjoy them.'

'Thank you, my lord.' Almost snatching them from his grasp, she made to leave the room, but at the door she hesitated, looking back at him uncertainly. 'The fact that you found me here with Gentile, despite your orders . . . it won't affect your promise to honour the agreement with my father?'

There was a lengthy pause before he replied, 'No, it won't affect my promise. Oddly enough, I believe you, Giulia. You couldn't possibly have known Gentile would be here.'

She breathed a sigh of relief. 'And you're not too angry with me for—for playing with him?'

He did not answer her question directly but half turned away to stare into the huge, empty fireplace. 'So you find my attitude unreasonable?'

Giulia said cautiously, 'I think you're too quick to see treachery, my lord, where often none exists. You seem to trust no one, not even your own family.'

'Come here,' he ordered peremptorily, and when she made no move he added in a quieter tone, 'There's no need to be afraid. I only want you to look more closely at this portrait.'

Giulia advanced slowly, unable to interpret his apparent change of mood. She sensed a curious tension in him and wondered how much this had to do with herself. Yet all his concentration was focused on the painting that hung above the mantelshelf, of the dark, unsmiling man whose features, she now saw, bore a striking resemblance to Pietro's own. Some distinguished ancestor, perhaps? Yet the clothes he wore were relatively modern.

'He was my father.' Pietro stared at the portrait with a strange intensity. 'Paolo Gabrieli.'

Giulia nodded. 'I should have guessed. You're very like him.'

'It was he who founded this library. He was a man of great wit and learning, a senator—and at one time a member of the Council of Ten.'

Giulia knew enough of Venetian politics to appreciate that Paolo Gabrieli must have wielded considerable power. All noblemen were members of the Greater Council, but the true rulers of the State were the elected Council of Ten, to whom even the Doge himself owed obedience. 'He must have been a remarkable man,' she murmured.

'Ay, too remarkable for his enemies.' Pietro's tone was bitter. 'He was murdered . . . stabbed to death in his own bed. And my mother strangled only a few yards away.'

'No!' Giulia turned white with shock. 'But who could have done such a terrible thing, and for what reason?'

Pietro continued to gaze at the portrait. 'They tried to prove he'd been plotting against the State,' he said tonelessly. 'But that was a lie. In fact the murderer was my uncle . . . his own brother. And the motive was envy.' He turned his head to look at her, his face without expression. 'And does it still surprise you that I see treachery everywhere? Even in my own family!'

Tears of compassion sprang into Giulia's eyes. She quickly lowered her lashes, trying to blink them away. 'No, my lord,' she murmured huskily. 'It doesn't surprise me.'

Without warning he put two fingers beneath her chin and lifted it up so that he could look down into her face. 'You're very pale,' he remarked. 'I hope I haven't frightened you too much?'

'No, I—I was pale before, from being so much indoors.' She feared this might sound like an accusation, and hurried to explain. 'In Verona I used to walk often in the open air, to run messages or go to the market. But here in Venice . . .' Her voice tailed away.

He dropped his hand from her chin and sighed. 'Well, I've no objection to your using the flat roof, if that would satisfy your craving for fresh air. Though I fear this is hardly the time of year for sitting out of doors.'

'The sun is shining today,' she said eagerly, pointing to the fingers of light slanting through the tall windows to lie across the floor. 'Oh, my lord! If I could only sit outside for a while, I *know* I should feel better.'

He gazed down at her animated face. Her brown eyes were suddenly aglow with anticipation, her red lips parted. 'Very well.' He placed both hands resolutely behind his back and turned again to stare into the fireplace. 'But you must take Zoe with you.'

'Yes, of course.' Fearful that he might yet change his mind, she began to edge towards the door. 'Thank you, my lord.'

He said nothing but raised his head to look once more at the portrait of his father, his head thrown back, his shoulders rigid. A solitary man, who would not allow himself to trust anyone for fear they might betray him. Giulia longed to utter some words of comfort, but it seemed as though he had forgotten her existence. Silently she left the room, to be escorted by Kasim back to her bedchamber.

The view from the flat roof of the Ca' Gabrieli was breath-taking. Leaning as far over the stone parapet as she dared, Giulia could see across the surrounding rooftops to the domes of St Mark's church, and beyond them the sweeping curve of the canal, sparkling in the winter sunshine. From here the city looked so beautiful that she found it difficult to believe it could be as full of danger and corruption as Pietro had described. Yet she knew that what he said was true. Venice's beauty was only skin deep: beneath the surface lay a hotbed of intrigue where no one could be sure who was his friend . . . or who his mortal enemy.

With a sigh she turned away and sat once more in a chair, while Zoe began to brush her still-damp hair. For this had seemed too good an opportunity to miss. As soon as Pietro had given her permission to sit outside she had sped back to her room and ordered Zoe to wash her hair so that it might dry in the sun. The flat roof, sheltered on two sides by the walls of the palazzo, proved surprisingly warm. Giulia loosened the neck of her caftan, baring her throat to the fresh air, and when Zoe was called away by another servant she took up the brush herself, applying it in long leisurely strokes until the silken strands began to shine like spun gold. At last she put down the brush and closed her eyes, drowsily raising her face to the sun.

This is Paradise, she thought, and then wondered why she felt so happy, for surely her situation was far from perfect. Yet it *had* changed—and changed for the better, she was certain. Pietro had allowed her to visit his library, he had not been angry when he found her playing with Gentile . . . and he had agreed to let her sit in the sunshine. All this must surely mean that he had at last begun to trust her.

But trust, she thought impatiently, was not enough! She wanted more than that. She wanted his love . . . The memory of her wedding night came vividly into her mind, the feel of his lips on hers, his body hard against her own. Suddenly she was overcome by such a wave of longing that she cried aloud and stretched out her arms beseechingly to the sun.

'By the rood!' said a low voice from close beside her. 'But you're a sight for sore eyes, Sister-in-law.'

Startled, Giulia wheeled round to see a pair of laughing eyes looking at her through the stone pillars of the parapet. 'Alessandro! But how did you . . . ?'

''Tis simple enough, when you know the way.' With practised ease he hoisted himself up until he was sitting astride the low wall and grinned at her impudently, swinging one elegant leg in its tight-fitting hose. 'By heaven,' he murmured, his light green eyes roving over her sun-warmed face and golden hair. ''Tis so long since I've seen you, I'd forgotten how beautiful you are!'

Giulia hastily pulled together the loosened fastenings of her caftan. 'You should not have come. What if someone finds you here?' She broke off, appalled by the realisation that all the good she had so far achieved would be undone . . . Pietro would never trust her again. She felt quite faint with dread.

'No fear of that,' Alessandro said confidently. 'My brother has gone to the Council Chamber, presumably to try and explain this further delay in his sailing.' He winked at her. 'Though I doubt he'll confess the true reason.'

'The true reason?' Giulia gazed at him uncomprehendingly.

'My dear Caterina, surely you must be aware that rumour is rife? Indeed, you're the talk of the town!'

She made an effort to conceal her alarm. 'You speak in riddles, Alessandro. I don't understand—what are these rumours?'

'Why, that you have my brother so enslaved that he cannot tear himself away from you.' He swung his other leg over the parapet and jumped lightly down. 'His ship was ready days ago, yet he's found a host of minor faults that he insists must be put right before he sails. The workers at the Arsenal say he does nothing but put obstacles in their way. Plainly he's reluctant to leave Venice, and one need not look far to find the reason why!'

Giulia was astonished. This was hardly the rumour she had expected to hear . . . nor indeed the rumour Pietro had been hoping to encourage, she was certain. 'I fear you're mistaken,' she said coolly. 'If Pietro is reluctant to leave Venice, it has nothing to do with me.' But even as she spoke, it occurred to her that Pietro might well be delaying his departure in order to start proceedings for the annulment of their marriage.

And that, moreover, could be the true reason for his visit to the Council Chamber . . .

Alessandro was quick to note the doubt in her eyes. 'You don't believe that,' he said softly, 'and neither do I. You're an enchantress, Caterina. No wonder my brother is so besotted that he keeps you locked in your room.' Without warning he dropped on one knee beside her and seized both her hands where they lay in her lap. 'Oh, the sweet irony of it! That he should think himself contracted to some prim country miss whom he must bed as a duty rather than a pleasure . . . and instead he finds himself wedded to a woman who would drive any man out of his senses.'

Alarmed by his ardour, Giulia shrank back. 'Are you mad? I warn you, my maidservant will return at any minute!'

'Don't worry about Zoe.' He gave a low laugh. 'I took the precaution of arranging for her to be kept safely out of the way so that I could be alone with you.' He slid an arm round her waist, pulling her closer. 'I wanted to sample those delights that have so bewitched my brother . . . and not only him, by all accounts.'

For a moment Giulia was too startled to move. Despite Pietro's warning, she had somehow not expected Alessandro to lay siege to her in quite such an obvious manner. At their previous meetings he had been flirtatious, but nothing more. Yet now he was regarding her with such a bold and knowing look that she was filled with dismay . . . and as his fingers wandered towards the unfastened opening of her gown her dismay turned to anger. She stood up, pushing him away so roughly that he lost his balance and fell backwards.

'How *dare* you!' She looked down at him with disgust. 'I'd thought you would show more respect towards your brother's wife.'

Agile as a monkey, Alessandro made a swift recovery. As Giulia turned to the door he leapt after her, catching hold of her arm. 'You play the virtuous woman most convincingly, Sister-in-law,' he muttered between gritted teeth. 'Yet I have it on good authority that you came to your wedding night by no means the innocent virgin you'd have us believe.'

Giulia stopped to stare at him. 'On *whose* authority?'

'One of your former lovers, no less.' His eyes were bright with malice. 'A young man from Verona—Bernardo by name—with whom I spent a most entertaining hour or so last evening.'

The colour drained from her face. '*Bernardo*'s here—in Venice?'

Alessandro smiled. 'He called at the house earlier in the day, but was turned away, by Pietro's orders. I followed him to the Falcon Inn, close by the Ponte di Rialto, where I found him seeking to drown his sorrows in Malvasey wine. He needed very little encouragement to tell me everything.'

'Everything?' Giulia repeated, her voice hardly more than a whisper.

Alessandro nodded, watching her face. 'The most touching tale, of two young lovers and their secret meetings in a candle-maker's house . . . and of the pleasures they enjoyed there—until, alas, his mistress was forced by her parents to marry another man.'

She shook her arm free of his grasp, detesting the crude insinuation in his voice. 'But why has he come to Venice?'

'To see you, of course!'

'That's impossible.' Her cheeks flushed with agitation. 'You must tell him so.'

'I've done my best, I assure you . . . But the poor fellow seems quite unable to believe that you are not as heartbroken as he is.' Alessandro heaved an affected sigh. 'Naturally I tried to convince him that you'd fallen deeply in love with my brother—so deeply, in fact, that you'd scarcely bothered to stir from the bedchamber since your wedding night. But he refused to accept that his Caterina could be so faithless.'

Giulia was silent, torn with indecision. If she agreed to see Bernardo he would recognise her at once, and heaven only knew what might be the consequences. Yet to send him away believing that Caterina no longer loved him would be cruel indeed. She could not live with it on her conscience.

'Only tell me where you wish to meet him,' Alessandro prompted slyly. 'And I will arrange it.'

'You know that I cannot leave this house.' Giulia frowned, thinking hard. 'How difficult is the climb up to this roof? Could Bernardo manage it as well as you?'

'A man in love can manage anything.' Alessandro smiled. 'Leave it to me, Sister-in-law.'

She said nervously, 'Please understand, I must see him alone.'

'I understand perfectly.'

Hearing the satisfaction in his voice, she realised with a qualm how greatly he would enjoy having her in his debt. 'I—I want only to persuade him that I'm happy in my marriage . . . and that he must return to Verona as soon as possible.'

'But of course!' Alessandro's eyes gleamed with

triumph. 'Shall we say tomorrow . . . at the same hour?'

She ran the tip of her tongue over lips that were suddenly dry. 'Yes, tomorrow . . . at the same hour.'

'You can rely on me to exercise the utmost discretion.' He swept her an exaggerated bow.

Before he had time to straighten, she slipped through the door. As she sped down the winding back staircase to the portego she made up her mind that she must somehow find a way to visit Caterina at the convent. Admittedly Ercole had forbidden her to attempt such a thing, but since then he had himself behaved unforgivably, refusing to come back to Venice when summoned by Pietro. She felt she owed her father nothing, least of all her obedience. And she *must* find out what Caterina wanted her to do—whether to send Bernardo away or to tell him the truth about the coming child. The decision was too difficult for her to take alone. She *had* to know Caterina's own wishes in the matter . . .

At the foot of the steps she met Zoe hurrying towards her at such a speed that they almost collided. Giulia put out a hand to steady the servant-girl and was astonished to find her trembling uncontrollably.

'Why, Zoe . . . whatever is the matter? Has something frightened you?'

Speechlessly the girl shook her head, but her eyes above the veil were wet with tears and she clung to Giulia as if for reassurance. No doubt she realised that she had been called away on a fool's errand, Giulia thought, and feared Pietro's wrath for disobeying his orders.

Giulia smiled at her encouragingly. 'Come,

there's no harm done. I'm perfectly safe, as you can see. But it grows a little chilly on the roof. I think 'tis time we returned to the bedchamber.'

The girl's trembling subsided. Relief showed in her eyes, mingled with gratitude. She followed meekly as Giulia led the way.

When Pietro appeared later in the day he found Giulia reclining upon the divan, apparently engrossed in the *Decameron Nights*. 'They please you, then—these tales of faithless wives and nuns disporting themselves with their confessors?' he inquired sardonically.

She saw at once that he was in a dangerous mood, and her heart sank. This did not augur well for the granting of her request. None the less she managed to say lightly, 'I find them entertaining, my lord, if somewhat incredible.'

'You don't believe such things can happen in real life?'

Yesterday, she remembered with a stab of fear, he had turned Bernardo away from the door. Did he suspect that she was in some way implicated? Yet he had made no mention of the incident, and since then had allowed her to use the library, which must surely mean he was convinced of her innocence. She took courage from the thought.

'I fear I've too little experience of the world to speak with certainty on such matters.' With a modest smile she glanced up at him—and saw a look in his eyes that made her catch her breath. She had taken care with her appearance, hoping it might prove a useful aid to her powers of persuasion. Her hair, still soft and fragrant from its morning washing, lay in a cloud about her shoulders and the flowing gown of soft white silk clung seductively to her figure. That Pietro was by no means immune to her attraction she knew already, but his expression now was such a strange mixture of anguish and desire that she hardly knew what to make of it.

So long did he remain gazing silently down at her that she grew nervous and sought to break the spell. 'Well, my lord, do you not think I look a little healthier for my hour in the sunshine?'

At this he turned away and went to stare out of the window. Giulia was seized by an even greater fear. Had he somehow learned of Alessandro's visit to the flat roof? Could this be the reason for his odd behaviour?

But almost at once he swung round and said abruptly. 'I've today set in motion proceedings for the annulment of our marriage.'

So her guesswork had been right! Even so, the words hit Giulia like a blow, robbing her of the power to speak. She stared at him, her eyes wide with shock.

'Why do you look at me like that?' he demanded. 'You knew well enough what I intended to do. This situation is intolerable, as you must surely realise, The sooner 'tis ended the better.'

She moistened her lips. 'Yes, my lord . . . you're right. 'Tis no more than I expected.'

He came closer, standing with his back to the light so that she could no longer see his face. 'I don't mean to throw you out on the street, if that's what troubles you. Since your father is clearly taking no further interest in your welfare, you must be my responsibility, whether I like it or not.'

His anger, Giulia realised, was only partly directed towards herself. It was almost as if he felt guilty at having taken such a step . . . yet he seemed resolute enough, she could not delude herself about that.

'What will you do with me, my lord?' she inquired humbly.

''Tis too early to say. I've not decided.'

She guessed from his tone that this was untrue. He had already decided, but was unwilling to tell her. Was it to be the convent for her as well?

The thought of the convent served as a reminder. With relief, she turned her mind to the more immediate problem of Caterina and Bernardo. 'I've something to ask of you, my lord,' she began tentatively.

'I warn you, you shall not make me change my mind.'

''Tis nothing to do with the annulment,' she said hastily. 'But with Caterina . . . 'Tis such a strange life she leads, cut off from her family and friends. Will you permit me to visit her?'

He seemed taken aback. 'You wish to visit Caterina?'

'Surely it's not such a surprising request? We were very close—as children we were constantly together and told each other everything—our inmost thoughts . . .'

'Is that what you wish to do now—confide in her your inmost thoughts?'

She was stung to retaliate. 'And if I do, what possible harm could there be? Caterina knows the truth—and is as much a captive in her way as I am! For both of us 'twill be a relief to speak freely to someone who understands.' She swung her legs off the divan, unheeding of the book that slipped from her lap to the floor, and stood before him. 'I beg you—let me go to her?'

He looked down at her face for a long moment,

then said resignedly, 'I'd forgotten how you women love to prattle.' He stooped to pick up the book and handed it to her. 'Very well, you may visit Caterina.'

'Thank you.' Tears of relief sprang into her eyes. 'Will you tell Kasim, so that he can take me to the convent?'

'That won't be necessary.' His eyes rested thoughtfully on her upturned face. 'I shall accompany you myself.'

CHAPTER SEVEN

THEY ARRIVED at the landward entrance of the convent, set in the narrow street close by St Mark's Square.

'You'd best go in alone,' Pietro said. 'I've no wish to eavesdrop on your girlish confidences.' When Giulia looked at him in surprise, he added, 'I'll wait for you at the end of this street. There are plenty of sideshows to keep me amused, so you need not hurry.'

This was even better than she had hoped. Indeed, his apparent reluctance to encounter the Prioress made her wonder if he were not suffering some pangs of conscience. Was he perhaps afraid that Mother Maria Innocenti might persuade him to let the marriage stand?

But as the heavy door closed behind her, she told herself this was wishful thinking. Pietro was firm in his resolution, she had no reason to doubt that. Moreover, these were selfish thoughts. She was here for Caterina's sake and must put all else out of her mind.

In the high, vaulted audience chamber she faced the Prioress, whose fine eyes regarded her gravely.

'I wished to see Caterina . . .' Giulia hesitated, filled with sudden doubt. Supposing Caterina was by now reconciled to becoming a nun? Would it be wrong to tell her that Bernardo was here in Venice in case she found the news unsettling? For a moment Giulia was tempted to confess the true purpose of her visit and ask for advice. Yet there was something about Mother Maria's cool, serene countenance that stopped her from speaking frankly. What could a nun possibly understand of love? Such emotions were too remote from her cloistered existence.

'The eastern style of dress suits you well,' the Prioress remarked unexpectedly. 'I assume you wear it in deference to your husband's wishes?'

'Why, yes . . .' Flushing, Giulia glanced down at the richly embroidered caftan that covered her from neck to toe. 'It—it pleases him that I should do so.'

'And do *you* please him, Giulia? Or is he angry with you for attempting to deceive him?'

Giulia stared at her. 'You guessed?'

The Prioress sighed. 'I never for one moment thought your father's plan would succeed. But I'd hoped Pietro Gabrieli might come to accept you for your own qualities of beauty and character.'

'I fear not.' Giulia set her chin at a defiant angle. 'Because I'm the daughter of a whore, he assumes that I must be of a similar disposition and therefore not fit to be his wife.' When the Prioress made no comment, she continued, 'He's seeking an annulment. Until then I'm kept a prisoner in my room and allowed to speak to no one, not even the members of his own family. He agreed to bring me here today only because he thinks there can be no harm in my talking to Caterina.'

'He's here?'

'He waits for me outside.'

The Prioress frowned. 'Giulia, if you don't wish

to return to him, I can offer you sanctuary. He cannot force you to leave the convent against your will.'

Giulia was taken aback. A faint blush stained her cheeks. 'No, I—I must return to him. You see, I've come to love him . . . and I cannot give up hope that he may change his mind.'

'That doesn't surprise me,' the Prioress said calmly. 'Pietro Gabrieli is a fine man—though much embittered, I fear, by his experiences. You know that both his parents were cruelly murdered?'

Giulia nodded. 'He has told me of it.'

'He told you himself?' The Prioress raised finely arched eyebrows. 'I've never known him speak of it to anyone since the deed was done. It was that, I think, that drove him away from Venice, more than the death of his first wife. He turned his back on politics, refusing even to take his seat on the Council, and became instead a seafaring man. For a time he seemed to find a way of life that pleased him in the East, yet that too has apparently now lost its charm for him. I fear he may be an idealist, for ever seeking the impossible dream.' She looked at Giulia with sympathy. 'Perhaps that's why he won't let himself love you, Giulia. You're too much flesh and blood to fulfil his notion of the perfect wife.'

Giulia was silent. The picture Mother Maria had given her of Pietro was an entirely new one . . . and yet it explained so much that she had not been able to understand.

'Indeed,' the Prioress continued dryly, 'I doubt very much if Caterina would have fulfilled it either.'

Caterina!

Giulia felt ashamed. In talking of her own troubles, she had almost forgotten why she had come. 'Is my sister well?' she asked. 'I've thought of her so much.'

'I'm afraid she's far from well,' Mother Maria said sombrely. 'Two days ago I sent for her father to come from Verona. He's with her now.'

'My father's *here*?' Giulia was stunned. 'But when Pietro summoned him, he would not come. He's sent no word to me at all!'

'No doubt he meant to call upon you as soon as he was able to leave Caterina's bedside.' Mother Maria turned to the door. 'If you wish to see her, she's in the infirmary.'

Giulia followed the Prioress through silent corridors to a bare, comfortless chamber containing six narrow beds. Only two were occupied; one by an elderly sleeping nun and the other by a wraithlike creature she could barely recognise as Caterina.

Ercole Tebaldi was kneeling at his daughter's bedside, his face grey with weariness. He looked up as they approached, showing neither surprise nor embarrassment at the sight of Giulia. 'I think she knows me,' he said, 'but she will not speak.'

'She's said very little since the day she arrived,' said the Prioress.

'I don't understand it.' Ercole shook his head. 'What ails the child?' He seemed quite unable to comprehend the depth of Caterina's feelings.

Giulia felt a rush of impatience towards this insensitive man she still found difficult to think of as her father. She said coldly, 'I'd like to speak to her alone.' Turning to the Prioress, she added, 'Please . . . 'tis very important.'

Mother Maria gave her a searching look. 'I see no harm, if you can bring her comfort.'

'I believe I can.'

The Prioress held her gaze for a moment longer,

then stooped to take Ercole's arm and help him to his feet. 'Come, you must rest,' she told him gently. 'We can safely leave Caterina in Giulia's care for a little while.'

He allowed himself to be led away, but stopped at the door to look back at the motionless figure lying upon the bed. 'I don't understand it,' he muttered again. 'She wanted to come here. She agreed it would be for the best.'

As soon as they had gone, Giulia crouched beside the bed and took Caterina's limp, cold hand in her own. She was no longer in any doubt as to what she must do. Her sister's pale face and dull sunken eyes told her all she needed to know. 'Listen to me,' she said urgently. 'Bernardo is here—in Venice. He came yesterday to the Ca' Gabrieli and asked to see you.'

Caterina gave no sign that she had even heard. Only the gentle snoring of the elderly nun broke the silence in the room.

'Can't you understand what I'm trying to tell you?' Giulia said despairingly. *'Bernardo is here!'*

Very slowly Caterina turned her head. Her lips moved almost imperceptibly. 'Ber-nardo?'

'Yes!' Giulia squeezed her hand tightly, as if willing her back to life. 'And tomorrow he comes again. I've arranged to meet him in secret—but first tell me, honestly, do you still love him?'

'I—love him . . .' The shadowed eyes filled with tears.

'And he loves you! But he believes you are married to Pietro Gabrieli. He doesn't yet know that I've taken your place. When he sees me, of course he'll realise what's happened and ask where you are. That's why I *must* know what you want me

to do. Do you want me to send him away—or tell him where he can find you?'

Miraculously the colour was beginning to return to Caterina's face. She tried to raise her head from the pillow. 'Tell him . . .'

'Yes?'

'Oh, what's the use!' Defeated, she slumped back. 'I have no strength . . .'

'You'll soon regain your strength . . . You *must*, for the sake of your child—and for Bernardo.' Giulia bent closer, speaking in a low, insistent tone. 'If I tell him the truth, he'll come at once and take you away. You can go to a town where no one knows you and be married before the baby is born.'

'My father will not allow it.'

'Your father needn't even know! But first you must convince him you're better. Then he'll go back to Verona and leave you alone. Come, try to sit up . . .' Giulia put her arm round Caterina and lifted her higher in the bed. She was shocked to discover how weak her sister had become. The once-shining hair hung in lank strands about her face. To cover her emotion she said brightly, 'You'll have to make yourself look beautiful before Bernardo sees you.'

Caterina stared at her, a frown creasing her brow. 'But if he comes here, they'll turn him away. The Prioress won't allow him to see me.'

'She will, if she thinks it may aid your recovery.' Giulia spoke with more confidence than she felt. 'She's not an unreasonable woman. She may even agree to help you.'

'But she's a friend of my father's . . .'

'Stop making difficulties!' She spoke so sharply that the elderly nun in the opposite bed momentarily stirred and gave a snort. Giulia waited until the snoring resumed before going on. 'You must make up your mind. Do you want to marry Bernardo and be happy with him for the rest of your life—or not?'

A spark of hope lit up Caterina's eyes, transforming her whole expression. Wordlessly she nodded.

'Then remember—*your* part is to convince your father you're quite recovered . . . and *mine* is to tell Bernardo where to find you.'

'Giulia . . .' Caterina spoke the name wonderingly, as if she had only just recognised her. 'You're so much changed, I . . .' She broke off, her eyes going to the door.

Giulia turned quickly. The Prioress stood only a few feet away from her, wearing her customary look of calm detachment. She must have entered the room silently . . . but when? How much had she heard of their conversation?

'I'm glad to see you looking so much better, Caterina,' said Mother Maria. 'But you mustn't overtire yourself. In a while I'll send your father in to see you again. For the moment I want Giulia to come with me.'

There was no mistaking the note of command in her quiet voice. Giulia pressed her sister's hand in an unspoken message of encouragement and followed the Prioress from the room.

Outside in the corridor Mother Maria turned to Giulia, her expression enigmatic. 'Almost a miracle,' she remarked dryly. 'I had thought to lose both mother and child . . . but instead it seems I'm to lose only a nun.'

So she had heard everything . . . and understood. Giulia felt as though a weight had been lifted from her back. Her eyes shone with gratitude but, before she could utter a word, the Prioress moved away, as if to discourage any exchange of confidences.

'Come,' she said. 'Let us break the glad news to your father.'

'She's recovered already?' Ercole stared incredulously from one to the other. 'But she seemed near to death . . .'

'Appearances can be very deceptive,' observed the Prioress. 'She had fallen into a melancholy, perhaps for lack of livelier company than we can provide here at the convent. Fortunately, the sight of Giulia has restored her spirits.'

'They were always close, though I hadn't realised Caterina set such store on the friendship.' Delighted, Ercole bestowed a beaming smile on Giulia. 'I was wrong to forbid you to visit her, my dear. You may come as often as you choose.'

'Giulia knows she will always be welcome here,' Mother Maria said smoothly. 'Now, if you'll excuse me, 'tis almost time for Vespers.' At the door she turned to address Ercole. 'When you've seen Caterina again you'll no doubt be leaving soon for Verona to tell your wife the good news, so I will bid you farewell.' Her gaze flickered briefly to Giulia before she left the room.

'Wonderful woman!' Ercole exclaimed, staring after her. He turned to Giulia, flinging his arms wide. 'And you, my dear, are in radiant health, I'm glad to see.' He embraced her fondly, seeming not to notice her lack of response. 'And what of your husband? He's already sailed for the Levant, I trust?'

Giulia stared at him disbelievingly. 'But did you

not receive the message he sent you, that you were to return immediately to Venice?'

Ercole had the grace to look discomfited. 'I received some such message, yes . . . but I was busy at the time. It wasn't convenient.'

'Not *convenient*?' Giulia felt her colour rising. 'Surely you realised how angry he would be when he discovered we'd deceived him?'

'At first, perhaps.'

'Pietro Gabrieli isn't the sort of man whose anger blows hot and cold.' She was so furious that she began to pace the audience chamber. 'And even if you weren't concerned about *me*, I'd have thought at least that you might show some interest in your trade agreement!'

'That's business,' Ercole declared obstinately. 'He wouldn't allow personal feelings to intrude upon a matter of trade.'

''Tis clear you've no conception what manner of man he is!' Giulia stared at her father helplessly. Though by no means stupid, he had little imagination, she realised. Her fury began to subside. 'Fortunately, I was able to make a bargain with him. Provided I do exactly as I'm told, he will honour his agreement with you.'

Relief showed plainly on Ercole's transparent face. 'That's excellent news.'

''Tis far from excellent for me!' Giulia retorted. 'I'm virtually a prisoner at the Ca' Gabrieli . . . and now he has begun proceedings for the annulment of our marriage.'

To her amazement, Ercole began to smile. 'Oh, come—he cannot possibly do that! He would have to provide medical proof.' He broke off at the sight of her flushed face. 'Are you trying to tell me that he . . . that you . . . ?'

'Tis not my fault, I assure you!' She turned away to hide her embarrassment. 'Heaven knows, I've shown myself willing enough.'

'Then what's wrong with the man?' Ercole's black brows drew together in a perplexed frown. 'You're a comely enough wench. I can hardly believe you're not to his taste?'

''Tis not that he finds me unattractive, I think . . . but he cannot bring himself to overlook the circumstances of my birth.'

If he heard the note of reproof in her voice, Ercole gave no sign of it. 'Well, if he finds you attractive, the remedy surely lies in your own hands? No man can resist a beautiful woman once she's made up her mind to ensnare him.' He beamed at her encouragingly. 'You must seduce him, my dear.'

'But he's leaving at any day . . .'

'Then you've not a moment to lose.' He pinched her cheek playfully. 'Be resourceful, Giulia! Now I must return to Caterina.'

As the door closed behind him she stood still, trying to stifle her resentment. Clearly her father had not changed one iota. He showed no remorse at having placed her in such an impossible situation, nor did it occur to him that the blame for Caterina's sickness could be laid partly at his own door. Once he was assured she was on her way to recovery, he would return to Verona with a clear conscience and most likely give no further thought to either of his daughters.

Well, wasn't that what she wanted? She had achieved what she set out to do . . . and now had only to tell Bernardo that Caterina loved him still.

As for the advice Ercole had given her with regard to Pietro—that was easier said than done!

*   *   *

When she emerged from the convent, she thought at first he had given up waiting for her. Then she saw him a little distance away, talking to a woman, and there was something in their attitude—the woman's hand upon his arm, his head bent close to hers—that Giulia found disturbing. Indeed, they seemed so engrossed in each other that she was able to approach them unnoticed till she was close enough to overhear their conversation.

'. . . just an intimate little gathering at my house,' the woman was saying. She was richly gowned in green velvet and wore a jewelled mask.

'I know well your intimate gatherings!' Pietro sounded sceptical, faintly amused.

'My dear, 'tis so long since I've seen you.' The woman tightened her grip persuasively. 'Come tomorrow night . . . and let me help you forget what troubles you.'

''Tis a tempting thought . . .' At this point he seemed to become aware of Giulia's presence, and drew back a little.

The woman was quick to take the hint. Unhurriedly she removed her gloved hand from Pietro's arm, murmuring, 'Till tomorrow, then . . .' Without even glancing in Giulia's direction, she moved away with a graceful, gliding walk that was somehow familiar.

Laura Rocco!

The courtesan whom Alessandro had described as the most famous in Venice, renowned for her wit and beauty . . .

And Pietro had virtually agreed to visit her house the next evening so that she might 'help him forget what troubled him'! A wave of jealousy swept over Giulia, quickly followed by suspicion. Was this why he had chosen to wait outside the convent, perhaps in the hope of meeting the beautiful courtesan?

She was so busy with her thoughts that when Pietro asked her a question she did not even hear him, and he was forced to repeat it. 'Your sister?' he said patiently. 'I trust you found her well?'

'Alas, no.' She tried to pull herself together. 'I fear that convent life does not agree with her. However, she seemed a little better for my visit.'

'I'm glad to hear it.' He placed a hand beneath her elbow, guiding her along the narrow street.

Her mind was in a turmoil as they made their way through the crowds in St Mark's Square to the waiting gondola. She longed to ask him about Laura Rocco, and yet could not summon the courage. On the return journey to the Ca' Gabrieli she kept as aloof from him as possible within the cramped cabin, staring miserably ahead.

'You seem upset,' Pietro remarked, his watchful eyes on her face.

'Is that so surprising? I'm worried about Caterina. She's very unhappy.'

'Surely that's no one's fault but her own,' he said unsympathetically. 'She has been indiscreet, and now she must pay the price.'

Giulia controlled her anger only by a supreme effort of will. 'How fortunate you are to be a man,' she murmured, 'for it seems to me that men may be as indiscreet as they please without ever having to pay for it.'

Ignoring her taunt, he made no further attempt at conversation. The silence between them lengthened. Was he already thinking of tomorrow night, she wondered, and the pleasures he would undoubtedly enjoy in the company of so accomplished a courtesan as Laura Rocco?

She returned to her bedchamber feeling chilled

and depressed, and ordered Zoe to prepare a bath in the hope that it might restore her spirits. While the servant-girl hurried away to do her bidding, she discarded her caftan and sank listlessly on to the divan to wait until the water was warmed.

A timid knocking at the door made her sit up, immediately alert. Who could it be? Surely Kasim would turn them away . . . unless . . . ?

Moving swiftly across the room, she opened the door. Gentile stood there, his eyes large with apprehension, while behind him towered Kasim, his dark face a study of conflicting emotions. Like many big men, she realised, he was at a loss when confronted by a small child. She was quick to take advantage of the fact.

'It's all right, Kasim. Gentile may enter.' Before the Turk could object, she pulled the boy inside and closed the door, smiling at him conspiratorially. 'You came to see me? I'm so glad.'

Gentile's eyes were fixed on her face. 'We play again?' he said in his low, hoarse voice. 'You hide . . . and I will count.'

But even before they could begin, the door burst open and Monna Clarissa stood upon the threshold, her thin face white with anger. Gentile at once threw himself against Giulia, clutching at her robe.

'This is the second time he has disobeyed me!' Monna Clarissa announced. 'Yesterday . . .'

'Yesterday we played a game,' Giulia intervened, placing a protective arm about Gentile's shoulders. 'That's why he came to find me again.'

But Monna Clarissa's eyes had slid past her to the bedchamber, widening as she saw the sumptuous oriental furnishings, the low bed suggestively veiled by gauzy curtains. 'This is a filthy, decadent place,' she declared, her voice shaking with emotion. 'Enough to contaminate the mind of a young child beyond redemption!'

Giulia was so startled by her vehemence that she offered no resistance as Monna Clarissa literally plucked Gentile from her grasp and pressed his face to her skirt, as if to protect his eyes from the evil sight.

Her shocked gaze swept over the clinging, transparent folds of Giulia's robe. 'As for you, madonna, you should be ashamed to show yourself so indecently clad before a child. Be assured my nephew the Cardinal shall hear of this!' So saying, she whisked Gentile away and down the corridor.

The whole incident had taken place at such speed that Giulia was left completely stunned. Her eyes met those of Kasim, who had been equally taken by surprise. 'There's no need to inform your master,' she said evenly. ' 'Tis not of sufficient importance.'

She closed the door and turned back into the room that had so offended Monna Clarissa. How surprised that virtuous lady would be, she thought ironically, to know that the occupant of these voluptuous surroundings lived as chaste an existence as her own! The scene had been almost farcical, yet it had ruffled her. She feared there might be reprisals for Gentile, and doubted whether he would ever attempt to visit her again.

She spent longer than usual in the bath, hoping it would soothe away the trials and frustrations of the day. The warm, fragrant water caressed her body, bringing at least a temporary easing of her tension. She closed her eyes and allowed herself to drift gently, lulled into a state of semi-consciousness.

It was not until the water began to grow cold that

she stirred and opened her eyes. To her consternation she saw Pietro standing at the side of the bath, watching her. How long had he been there? Her first thought was that he had somehow heard of the unfortunate incident with Monna Clarissa and meant to reprimand her, but then she saw a light burning in his eyes that drove all other considerations from her mind.

No man can resist a beautiful woman once she's made up her mind to ensnare him, Ercole had said. *You must seduce him, my dear.*

With deliberate slowness she climbed out of the bath, aware that the water streaming over her naked body turned her skin to liquid gold. At the top of the steps she posed for an instant, allowing his eyes to feast on her beauty, then languidly raised a hand to unfasten the hair pinned on top of her head and let it fall about her glistening shoulders.

He stood immobile, his gaze holding hers intently.

'My lord,' Giulia murmured huskily, 'since you seem to have sent Zoe away, then you must take her place. Will you hand me a towel?'

As if mesmerised, he took the soft white towel from the bench and held it out, still not moving from the spot where he stood. Giulia walked towards him, her every movement charged with conscious allure. Then, in an act of calculated provocation, she turned her back and lifted her arms in an unspoken command for him to wrap the towel around her.

After a moment's hesitation, he obeyed. 'Now dry me,' she commanded, holding her breath for fear he might refuse.

Slowly he began to rub the towel against her

body, the gentle friction bringing a warm glow to her skin. She felt a delicious languor stealing over her and with a little sigh allowed herself to melt against him, leaning back until her head rested on his shoulder. For a second he froze, then resumed his slow, rhythmical massage, moving the towel in circles over the uplifted contour of her breasts. Giulia felt an almost unbearable ache of desire begin to grow within her. Her body responded eagerly to the increasingly urgent pressure of his hands and she sensed that he too was aroused, his breath coming warm and fast against her neck, his hands no longer careful to keep the towel between them. But as his warm fingers closed over her naked breast she felt something metallic rasp against her skin and, looking down, saw it was the gold ring of approval. She gave a little cry of shock, breaking the spell of sensuality that held them both in thrall, and in a single, lithe movement twisted within the circle of the towel to press herself against him, winding her arms about his neck. 'Oh, my lord—you cannot be so cruel! I beg you, end this constraint between us . . .'

She felt his lean body taut against her own and reached upwards to press her lips against the line of his jaw. 'I'll not betray you, I swear it, but will play the part of Caterina so well no one will ever guess. Even my hands won't give me away. Feel how soft they are now . . . like rose petals . . .'

'It's no use, Giulia!' Roughly he pushed her away from him. 'You cannot fool me so easily. I know well enough what is your plan. You seek to trick me out of the annulment.'

She caught the towel as it threatened to slip from her altogether. 'But don't you understand? I *love* you!' As soon as the words had escaped, she wished them unsaid. They left her vulnerable, her spirit as naked as her body.

He seemed unimpressed by the revelation. 'Oh, for a while you almost had me convinced that you were different from other women. You'd even begun to trouble my conscience!' He gave a short laugh. 'Until tonight's little performance. This has been most enlightening.'

She blushed hotly. 'I only wanted . . .'

'You made it perfectly clear what you *wanted*, my dear!' His tone was mocking. 'And I'm flattered, I assure you. Indeed, it seems to me that the sooner we free ourselves of this ridiculous marriage the happier we both shall be.'

Tears of frustration sprang into her eyes. '*You* may be free,' she said bitterly. 'But I see little happiness for me, shut away behind the high walls of a convent.'

'A convent? What put that idea into your head?'

'You said you had plans for me . . .'

'So I have. But they certainly don't include sending you away to become a nun!' His glittering eyes roved over the pale gold body so inadequately covered by the towel she was still clutching to her breasts. 'That would be a criminal waste of your charms.'

She stared at him, her mouth suddenly dry. 'Then what . . . ?'

'I shall buy you a house,' he said carelessly, 'where I may visit you as often as I please.'

'You would make me a *whore*?'

'Why so shocked? 'Twas your mother's profession, after all.' His expression softened as he looked at her. 'Nature might have fashioned you to be a courtesan, Giulia. You have all the attributes—beauty, intelligence . . . and doubtless certain other talents that can make a man forget his troubles.'

The words evoked an unwelcome memory of Laura Rocco . . . *I will help you forget what troubles you.*

Giulia flung back her head, challenging him. 'And what happens when you tire of me?'

'Oh, I don't doubt you'll find yourself another protector soon enough.' He raised her chin, looking down into her vivid, stormy face. ''Tis a solution that will suit us both, I think. But for the moment . . .' He broke off, releasing her abruptly. 'For the moment 'tis best we see each other as little as possible.'

'I didn't ask you to come and watch me bathing,' she retorted. A small suspicion came into her mind. 'And how many times before have you spied on me when I was in the bath . . . or sleeping?'

She saw him flinch and knew she had caught him out. Plainly he did not care to be reminded of his weakness—and she suspected that was exactly how he regarded his physical need of her . . . as no more than an unfortunate weakness to be kept in check until he was free to indulge it.

'Perhaps 'tis as well,' he said stiffly, 'that I've been ordered to sail on the day after tomorrow, on the evening tide.'

'The day after . . . ?'

But he was already striding from the room.

Later, when she was dressed and lying upon the divan, she picked up the *Decameron Nights* in the hope it might divert her restless mind. The book fell open at the story of a Frenchwoman whose husband declined to consummate their marriage because he was enamoured of another lady, and who declared that he would return to live with her only when she had his ring upon her finger and his son dandled upon her arm. Whereupon she had secretly taken the place of her husband's paramour in his bed and so pleased him that he was persuaded, all unknowingly, to part with his ring . . .

Giulia let the book slip from her hands.

Be resourceful, her father had said.

And tomorrow night Pietro would go to the house of Laura Rocco, still wearing the gold ring of approval on his little finger . . .

CHAPTER EIGHT

GIULIA ARRIVED on the flat roof a little earlier than the hour appointed for her meeting with Bernardo. She had lain awake half the night making plans and now was impatient to put them into action.

Her first task was to send Zoe away. She had a number of rather lame excuses ready, but a far better one presented itself in the shape of her silver-backed hairbrush still lying where she had left it the day before, on the ground beside the chair. Hastily she covered it with the hem of her caftan, and turned to Zoe.

'I've a fancy for you to tend my hair. 'Tis so soothing, and I've a slight headache. Go and fetch the brush.' She saw the alarm in the servant-girl's eyes, and added gently, 'You need not fear I shall come to any harm. Kasim stands guard at the foot of the stairs. Go quickly.'

With some reluctance, Zoe obeyed. It would take her a while to discover the brush was missing, Giulia thought, yet there was not a moment to lose. She leaned over the balcony to see the familiar figure of Bernardo already climbing awkwardly towards her, assisted from below by Alessandro. 'Hurry!' she called in a low voice.

A minute later Bernardo arrived, his round face scarlet with exertion. Although he had obviously bought a new suit of clothes to impress his beloved, and was colourfully clad in an apricot tunic over striped black and sky-blue hose somehow this peacock finery did not suit his stocky figure and honest burgher's face. Moreover he had torn the sleeve of his tunic on the ascent so that it now hung in tatters from his arm, though he seemed quite unaware of this mishap. 'Ah, Giulia!' he panted, his eyes going hopefully past her to the deserted roof. 'Where is your mistress?'

Giulia first made certain that Alessandro had waited below, well out of earshot, then told Bernardo what had happened at such speed that he was totally confused. She began again, more slowly, until at last he managed to grasp what she was trying to tell him, that Caterina was not in fact married to Pietro Gabrieli but was at the Convent of S. Cecilia, awaiting the birth of his child. 'You must go to her at once,' Giulia urged. 'Ask to see the Prioress. She knows the whole story and I believe will help you.'

'A child . . .' Bernardo said wonderingly, still some way behind in their conversation. '*My* child—but why was I kept in ignorance of this? Surely it was my *right* to know!'

'I haven't time to explain. Caterina will tell you everything when you see her.' Giulia glanced over her shoulder, fearful that Zoe would return at any minute. 'Now, Bernardo . . .'

'We shall be married! Caterina and I are to be married . . .' His eyes were shining as if he had just received some beatific vision.

'Yes, yes!' Giulia said impatiently. 'But *please* listen to me. I have a favour to ask of you.'

Bernardo's ecstatic gaze focused with some difficulty on her face. 'You're a good girl, Giulia,' he said generously. ' 'Twas a noble act to take

Caterina's place. Only tell me what I can do to repay you.'

'I want you to take a message to my sister-in-law, Francesca Massimo. She lives close by the Rialto bridge—any boatman will know where. You must contrive to speak to her alone. Tell her I wish to go out this evening, and I have nothing to wear.'

Bernardo's astonishment showed clearly on his guileless face. 'But won't this strike her as an odd request? Surely, as wife to Pietro Gabrieli, you have as many clothes as you could wish?'

'She won't be in the least surprised, I promise you. Only you must impress upon her that this is a secret. 'Tis essential no one else should know of it.' She saw that Bernardo was still mystified, and wondered how best to reassure him. So much depended upon his doing exactly as she asked. Then she remembered that he was a poet by nature, highly susceptible to a hint of romance. With a modest blush, she added, 'The truth is I'm planning a—a little surprise for my husband and don't wish him to guess my intentions.'

'Ah!' A fatuous smile spread over his face. 'I understand . . .'

'Now you must go.' Unceremoniously she began to hustle him off the balcony. 'And say no word of this to Alessandro. He thinks I'm Caterina and must not be disabused of the idea.'

'Very well.' Somewhat gingerly he began the descent.

'Oh, and Bernardo . . .' She leant over the parapet. 'I know you're anxious to see Caterina as soon as possible, but could you please go first to my sister-in-law? The matter is *very* urgent.'

His reply was muffled by the effort of sliding down a sloping roof to where Alessandro awaited him, and before she could repeat the question she heard the door open behind her. Rather than make a sudden guilty movement, she stayed where she was a moment longer, pretending to admire the view. 'Ah, Zoe,' she said, slowly turning her head, 'you've been so long, I . . .'

But it was Pietro who stood there, his eyes narrowed suspiciously. 'What are you doing here alone?' he demanded. 'Where is Zoe?'

'She's gone to fetch my hairbrush . . .' Her voice tailed away as she saw the silver brush where it lay on the ground between them, glinting in the sunlight.

Pietro picked it up and handed it to her. 'She'll have a fruitless search, it seems.'

'I must have left it there yesterday. How strange we hadn't noticed.' Casually she moved away from the parapet, aware that if Pietro looked over the edge he would undoubtedly catch Bernardo still making his perilous descent. She gave a little shiver. 'In fact 'tis colder out here than I'd realised.'

'No colder than yesterday.'

'None the less I think I shall return to my chamber.'

For a moment she thought he meant to bar her way; but as she walked towards him he stepped back, almost as though he was afraid to risk physical contact. Another second and she would have slipped through the door, but a sudden noise made them both turn round. To her horror she saw the top of Alessandro's head come into view as he hoisted himself level with the balcony.

'Well, sweet Caterina—are you not pleased with me?' He had already swung one leg over the parapet before he caught sight of Pietro. His green eyes widened in shock, but he recovered quickly, and said with mock dismay, 'Forgive me, Brother. I hadn't meant to intrude. 'Twas my intention merely to inquire after Caterina's state of health. 'Tis improved, I hope?'

'She's in excellent health, as you can see.' Pietro's tone was sharp as a knife-edge. 'And how many times before have you visited her here on the roof to express your concern?'

'Why, never!' The gleam in Alessandro's eyes made a mockery of his protestation. 'It isn't an easy climb, as you can imagine. This is the first time I've attempted such a feat.'

'*You're lying!*' His face thunderous, Pietro took a threatening stride towards his brother, whereupon Alessandro's bravado swiftly evaporated. With remarkable speed he swung himself off the balcony and dropped from sight.

Cheated of his prey, Pietro swung round to face Giulia. She had not moved, her face frozen in a mask of apprehension. For an instant he studied her in silence, then roughly seized her by the wrist and pulled her after him through the door.

The suddenness of his action startled her out of her stupor. 'My lord, I can explain . . .'

But he paid no heed, half-dragging her down the winding flight of stone steps to where Kasim stood on guard, and along the corridor, his fingers biting into her flesh. When they reached her chamber, he thrust her so violently through the door that she almost fell at Zoe's feet.

'Your mistress has found her hairbrush,' Pietro said coldly. 'Take it from her and put it where it cannot be so easily mislaid.'

Zoe did as she was told, keeping her eyes averted from Giulia's flushed face, and disappeared through the concealed door.

Pietro went on grimly, 'How near you came to making a fool of me! It must give you great satisfaction.'

Giulia shook her head, rubbing her bruised wrist. 'That was not my intention.'

'Oh, spare me that look of virtuous honesty, the trembling lip! They no longer have the power to move me.' The contempt in his voice made her wince. 'Twice now you've betrayed yourself for what you are—a harlot who would give herself to any man if she thought it would further her own ends. No doubt you wished to keep Alessandro dangling in case you had need of a second string.'

'That's not true!'

'Well, you may indeed have need of him, for you've forfeited any right you had to *my* benefaction! As soon as we're legally free of each other, you may go upon the streets for all I care. I would not touch you if you were the last woman left in Christendom!' He all but snarled the final words, then turned on his heel and left the room.

Giulia stood rooted to the spot. She felt as though she were drowning in a sea of hopelessness, but as the waters threatened to close over her head she clutched at a single straw. *She had given Bernardo the message for Francesca!* In that at least she had succeeded, though heaven only knew if he would deliver it, since his mind was inevitably full of Caterina.

And even if he did remember to deliver it, would Francesca come? Once again the waters engulfed her. But from the very depths of despair was born a new resolution. She made up her mind that somehow she *would* escape . . . and visit the house of Laura Rocco tonight, no matter what the consequences.

After all, what had she left to lose?

It was almost dusk when there came sounds of a disturbance outside her bedchamber. Giulia, lying upon the divan, had been reading again and again the story of the Frenchwoman as though she would commit it to memory, but on hearing Francesca's voice she thrust the book guiltily beneath a cushion and rose to her feet, her heart pounding.

'That heathen creature is really quite impossible!' Francesca swept into the room with an air of bustling normality that blew like a fresh breeze through the oppressive atmosphere. 'He behaves as if he were the master and I the servant. I've just had to deal most firmly with him.'

Giulia gazed at her speechlessly, her fragile hopes crumbling into dust. For Francesca carried no bag, nothing that could possibly contain a change of clothing.

'My dear!' She took off her mask and advanced upon Giulia, her silken skirts rustling beneath a cloak of burnt-orange velvet edged with sable. 'I'm so *glad* you've sent for me at last—and all agog to know how I can help you. Your messenger told me that you wish to go out this evening, but that Pietro is not to know of it. Is this true?'

Giulia could only nod her head.

Francesca looked at her quizzically. 'Forgive me, but there's one question I must ask at once. Are you intending to meet a lover?'

'In a way . . .'

Francesca sighed. 'Well, I confess I'm not altogether surprised. Last time I came, it was clear that all was not as it should be between you and my brother. Even so, 'tis early days and I cannot imagine who . . .' She paled. 'It's not Alessandro, I hope?'

'No!'

'I'm relieved to hear it, for that would be most unwise. Then it must be your messenger. He told me he had known you in Verona but seemed unwilling to vouchsafe any further information. A pleasant young man, I thought, though somewhat provincial in his manners.'

''Tis not Bernardo either,' Giulia said quickly, anxious to put an end to Francesca's conjecturing. 'Tis Pietro himself I go to meet.'

'Pietro?' Francesca gazed at her, astonished. 'But where?'

'At the house of Laura Rocco.'

For a second Francesca was shocked into silence. Then she inquired, 'What makes you so certain Pietro will be there?'

'I overheard a conversation . . .' Even as Giulia spoke, it occurred to her that Pietro had not in so many words accepted the courtesan's invitation, yet in his present mood it seemed likely he would go, if only to vent his frustration with her upon someone else.

'And you wish to catch him out?' Francesca frowned. 'My dear, husbands are all the same. In my experience 'tis far better to close one's eyes to such things. A courtesan, after all, presents no real threat to a wife.'

'You misunderstand.' Giulia blushed. 'I—I wish to play a trick on him, that's all.'

Francesca looked intrigued. 'What kind of a trick?'

Giulia's blush deepened. 'I want him to make love to me without knowing who I am.'

Francesca gave a little shriek of mirth, quickly

stifled. 'To seduce one's own husband . . . what a novel idea! And to visit the house of Laura Rocco . . . Why, they say 'tis most luxuriously appointed and her collection of paintings one of the finest in Venice.' Her eyes sparkled. 'I've half a mind to come with you!'

Giulia was alarmed. 'No, please—'tis most important I go alone.'

Francesca shot her a curious glance. 'You seem to be taking this all very seriously. 'Tis no more than a joke, surely?'

'Of course!' Giulia made an effort to sound light-hearted.

Without warning, Francesca caught hold of Giulia's hand. She saw that the ring of approval was still missing, and said shrewdly, 'Are you being entirely honest with me, Caterina? I think perhaps you may have a more devious motive . . .'

Giulia snatched her hand away and hid it behind her back. 'I don't know what you mean. Why else should one want to seduce one's own husband, save as a joke?'

'In my case it would be more of a miracle than a joke,' Francesca said with a sigh of regret. 'But how will you persuade Laura Rocco to let you enter her house? I warn you, a courtesan doesn't take kindly to wives who pursue their husbands over her threshold!'

'She will not object, I think, if I tell her I'm pursuing someone else's husband. I shall say I'm married to a man who neglects me and have come to her house in search of some diversion. Surely such a thing cannot be so unusual in Venice, especially at Carnival time?'

'No-o,' Francesca admitted reluctantly. 'Even so, I think you're taking a risk. Pietro may be very angry when he recognises you.'

'I don't intend that he *should* recognise me.'

'But how will you disguise yourself?'

'I shall wear a mask. As to my clothes, I was hoping you'd bring me something to wear. Bernardo cannot have given you the whole of my message.'

'Now that's where you're wrong!' Francesca's eyes began to sparkle again. 'Had you not noticed how plump I've become all of a sudden?' She took off her cloak to reveal yet another cloak of anonymous black, and beneath it a loose-fitting dress of blue damask. 'Unfasten the buttons,' she ordered, turning her back.

Giulia helped her sister-in-law out of the blue dress to discover that beneath it she wore a gown of green brocade embroidered with gold thread and glittering gems.

'There!' said Francesca triumphantly, turning round to display herself. 'Is this not a gown you can happily wear tonight at Laura Rocco's? And, I promise you, Pietro has never set eyes on it. Quick—help me take it off. I cannot wait to see how well it suits you.'

Giulia obeyed. Her hands were shaking as she stepped into the green brocade gown. Now that her plan looked like becoming a reality her numbness began to recede and she felt alive again, tingling with anticipation.

'Draw in your breath while I fasten the bodice,' Francesca ordered. 'You are more generously proportioned than I, but that's hardly surprising, since you're somewhat taller. I only hope the gown is long enough . . .' She stood back, critically surveying Giulia's appearance. ''Tis a little on the short side, but I think no one will be looking at your feet!'

Giulia flushed self-consciously. The gown was daringly cut, Francesca's own taste being for the unashamedly flamboyant, and the tight-fitting bodice pushed up her breasts so that they swelled provocatively above the low neckline. Strangely she felt more naked than in any of the eastern robes she had been wearing, yet she told herself that her appearance was entirely in keeping with the rôle she had to play. In a room full of courtesans she would pass unremarked.

'Now your hair,' said Francesca. 'Nothing too elaborate, I think, but a style Pietro will not immediately recognise.' She set to work, coiling the silken tresses into the nape of Giulia's neck and enclosing them within a net of fine gold mesh she took from her own hair.

'This is all very fine,' Giulia said. 'But how am I to leave the house? Kasim is constantly on guard.'

'Nothing simpler,' Francesca assured her. 'If you put on the mask and cloak I was wearing when I arrived, Kasim will take you for me and allow you to leave unchallenged. I fancy he's a little afraid of me!' She smiled. 'Go straight to the water-gate, where you will find my gondola. Instruct the boatman first to take you to the house of Laura Rocco, then to return here for me.'

'But when *you* come to leave, surely Kasim will know that he's been tricked?'

Francesca shrugged. 'By then it will be too late.'

And afterwards, Giulia thought, when she must return to the Ca' Gabrieli . . . what then?

Well, she would deal with that problem when it arrived. For the moment she must concentrate on achieving her immediate task . . . and leave the rest to Fate.

* * *

It was almost too easy. The burnt-orange cloak, so conspicuous in colour, fulfilled its function admirably. Kasim, assuming she was Francesca, had let her pass without a second glance. The boatman, too, seemed unsurprised by the appearance of another woman in his mistress's clothes and carried out her orders unquestioningly.

Apprehensive though she was of what lay ahead, Giulia could not fail to be entranced by the magic of Venice at night. Lanterns swung from the prows of other vessels gliding by in the silvery dark, and after a while her boatman, no doubt suspecting that he took part in some amorous adventure, burst into song. His voice had a harsh, broken quality that Giulia found intensely moving and, when he paused, his song was taken up by another gondolier . . . and another and another, passing the strange, haunting melody back and forth across the waters. She found herself wishing the journey could go on for ever, but all too soon the gondola bumped gently against a landing-stage and the boatman sprang to tie his vessel to a striped mooring-post.

Giulia stepped out, staring in wonder at the building rearing up before her. So this was the house of Laura Rocco! It was far grander than she had expected.

Two liveried footmen stood on either side of the doorway, but neither challenged her right to enter. She passed through as though in a trance, and climbed the marble staircase to the salon. On the way, she met a number of men and women, all masked like herself and fashionably dressed, but no one gave her more than a casual glance.

The salon, with its damasked walls and gilded couches, had an air of dignity that surprised her. None the less she was uneasily aware of an all-pervasive sensuousness in the atmosphere, the heady scent of the women who drifted past, leaning against their escorts while they conversed in hushed tones and occasionally breaking into low, suggestive laughter. A slow but steady flow of traffic moved in and out of the many rooms leading off the salon, and from somewhere in the distance came the sound of a lute.

When a servant came to remove her cloak she had no option but to part with it, even though it left her feeling naked and vulnerable. She received some curious glances, the men in particular regarding her with interest. The sooner she found Pietro the better, she thought, before she was caught up in a situation she could not control.

She saw him almost at once. He was standing at the far end of the salon, his height giving him the advantage of a clear view over the people surrounding him. Their eyes met with a kind of awful inevitability, as though there were no one else in the room, and he started towards her at once.

Giulia closed her eyes, feeling suddenly faint. What a fool I was, she thought, to imagine for one instant that I could deceive him! Of course he has recognised me—and now will make me suffer for my foolishness by public humiliation . . .

She sensed that he had come to stand before her and braced herself for an explosion. But nothing happened, and at length she opened her eyes to look at him.

He was staring at her intently. 'Tell me your name,' he said, his voice harsh and oddly constrained.

Giulia hesitated. Was it possible that he was not after all quite sure of her identity? Suspicious, perhaps, but not certain enough to denounce her outright. Yet, if she spoke in her normal voice, he would know her at once. She must find some way of disguising it . . .

'My name is Ginette,' she said, with a lilting accent. 'Ginette de Narbonne, from Paris.'

It was fortunate that Ercole Tebaldi had once employed a French sewing-maid, whose accent Giulia, a natural-born mimic, had loved to imitate. Curiously, she found that with the new voice she seemed also to have acquired a new personality, flirtatious and consciously alluring.

'And you, monsieur?' she inquired, deliberately pouting her full lower lip. 'How are *you* called—or do you prefer not to say?'

'Better it should remain a secret.' His gaze dwelt on her mouth, the only part of her face visible beneath the mask. 'I find you enchanting, mademoiselle.'

'Madame,' she corrected. 'But you will please to call me Ginette.'

'You're married?' He sounded not unpleased. 'And your husband—is he here this evening?'

'No, he is not!' She leant towards him confidentially. 'He is a very dull gentleman who neglects me shamefully. That is why I have come here tonight, hoping to find perhaps a little . . . excitement?'

Pietro's gaze left her parted lips and slid lower, to the rounded breasts so seductively revealed by her décolletage. 'By heaven, madame,' he said softly, 'I believe you may be the answer to my prayer, for I too have come in search of excitement, though in truth I hadn't expected to find it in so agreeable a form. Will you allow me to be your escort?' He held out his arm.

Giulia felt a quite unreasonable stab of jealousy.

That he should be so quickly attracted to an unknown Frenchwoman seemed almost insulting—and yet perversely she had begun to enjoy her role as Ginette de Narbonne. She put a hand on his arm, smiling up at him invitingly. 'Monsieur, I would like for you to be my escort. I think you are the handsomest man I have ever met.'

'How can you tell, when I am masked?' His voice was teasing.

'A mask deceives only the eye. 'Tis in her heart that a woman knows if a man is handsome or not.'

He laughed and led her further into the room, calling for wine. Giulia had never seen him so light-hearted. Again she felt resentful that he had never shown this side of his nature to her before. But as Ginette she pouted and smiled as they moved towards the supper-table, clinging to his arm and playing her part with some relish, though careful not to drink too much of the wine he was pressing upon her in case it befuddled her wits. Their conversation remained trivial, yet the words they spoke were important. It was as though they played a game, every move taking them nearer and nearer to the inevitable conclusion.

When they had eaten, they found a quiet corner and sank on to a couch. Pietro slid his arm along the back, leaning close to her. 'This husband who neglects you,' he murmured, his fingers brushing against her neck as if by accident. 'Is he blind?'

Giulia gave a Gallic shrug. 'I think perhaps he is a little short-sighted, yes.'

Pietro's eyes gleamed with triumph. 'Ah, then he's elderly!'

''Tis true this is his second marriage,' she said evasively.

'And he has little energy left to please his new

young wife?' He gave a low laugh. 'What a waste of so much beauty!'

'I too am masked,' she reminded him with a mischievous curve of her lips. 'So how can you be sure that I am beautiful?'

''Tis not only my heart that tells me so.' He leant closer still, his breath warm against her ear. 'I fear I'm growing impatient, Ginette. Would it please you that we should be alone?'

She turned her head to look at him. His eyes were glittering through the slits in his mask and his lips no longer smiling. She sensed his urgency, and knew with a sudden flash of intuition that he desired Ginette only because of her resemblance to Giulia.

'It would please me very much, monsieur,' she said quietly.

Their eyes met and held, but before either of them could move, a shadow fell across their faces and Laura Rocco stood before them. She alone of all the women in the room was unmasked, her lovely features set in an expression of cold displeasure.

'Well, my lord?' she said on a note of inquiry. 'Perhaps you'd better introduce me to this lady, since to the best of my knowledge I have never set eyes on her before.'

Undismayed, Pietro rose to his feet. 'In that case allow me to present Madame Ginette, a visitor from France.' He held out his hand to Giulia.

She hastily dropped a curtsy. 'Madame, forgive me. I come uninvited to your house—but I have heard your name so often since I came to Venice that I was eager to make your acquaintance.'

'How flattering,' said Laura Rocco with an ironical lift of her eyebrows.

'Madame Ginette has a dullard husband who finds himself unable to amuse her,' Pietro interposed smoothly, still keeping hold of Giulia's hand. 'That is why she came here this evening—to be amused.'

'Which I'm sure you've done most admirably, my lord.' Laura Rocco cast a professional eye over Giulia's face and figure as if assessing her attributes. 'You're very pretty, my dear. However, I prefer to know a good deal more about the guests in my house, so I regret I must ask you to leave.'

'If *she* leaves, then so do I.' Pietro's tone was uncompromising.

Her eyes flashed with annoyance, quickly concealed. 'My lord, aren't you being a little unreasonable? There are many other young women here this evening who I'm sure will be only too pleased . . .'

'This is the one I've chosen.' Pietro tightened his grip on Giulia's hand. 'No other will do.'

Laura Rocco stared at him for an instant. Then she gave a little shrug of resignation. 'Since you're so notoriously difficult to please, it seems I have no choice in the matter.' She looked again at Giulia. 'I take it Madame is willing?'

'She's willing,' he said confidently. 'We await only your co-operation, Laura, in finding us a room where we can be alone.'

The courtesan gave a light, brittle laugh. 'You must curb your impatience a little longer, my lord. Let Madame Ginette come with me.'

Reluctantly he released Giulia's hand. She dared not look at him again but followed the tall, graceful figure of Laura Rocco from the salon.

When they reached the upper floor, Laura stopped outside a door, but before opening it, she said, 'Tell me, what do know of this man?'

'Only that he has been kind to me,' Giulia replied, careful to maintain her French accent. 'And I—I am very much attracted to him.'

'And he to you, that's plain enough. You're very fortunate, my dear, to succeed where so many have failed. If you can keep him with you till morning, you'll have done very well.' She spoke bluntly, as if to one of her own kind. Giulia flushed a little behind her mask. 'But what of your husband? Will he not think it strange if you don't return to him tonight?'

'I have reason to believe he's otherwise engaged.'

'How convenient.' She flung open the door.

The room was already lit, though not to excess. In the flickering torchlight Giulia saw that the walls were hung with tapestries and the ceiling painted with scenes of naked gods and goddesses disporting themselves amidst the clouds. But her eyes were drawn inevitably to the enormous bed which stood on a dais, and behind it an ornate wooden headpiece painted gold.

'This is my best room,' said Laura Rocco. 'In the chest you will find something appropriate to wear. I'll give you a few minutes to prepare yourself before I send him to you.' At the door she hesitated. 'It seems to me you're very young and perhaps not too experienced in the ways of men, so let me give you some advice. Men are strange creatures and do not always come to us for the most obvious reasons. If he wishes to make love, give yourself freely. If he wishes to talk, don't try to stop him. For a man loves to boast of his prowess, and there's nothing pleases him better than a woman who listens.'

Giulia said nothing. No doubt the words were

kindly meant, but they only served to remind her of the devious rôle she had to play. Laura Rocco gave her a last, speculative look and left the room.

Now, suddenly, Giulia stood irresolute. The room oppressed her with its voluptuous paintings and gilded ornamentation. She felt a rising panic, and in an effort to suppress it opened the chest that Laura Rocco had pointed out. It contained several silken bed-gowns, all transparent and of so indecent a cut that she was filled with disgust and slammed down the lid. She would not resort to such methods!

However, she must 'prepare herself', as Laura Rocco had commanded. She tried to undo the buttons that fastened her bodice at the back but found it impossible to reach all of them. Her panic returned and she began to wish she had not come, that she was safely back in her chamber at the Ca' Gabrieli . . .

'Allow me to help you, madame,' said a familiar voice behind her.

Giulia had not even heard him enter the room. She stood immobile while his fingers made short work of the buttons and slid the gown from her shoulders till she was naked to the waist. He pulled her back against him, cupping her pointed breasts in his hands, and murmured something against her neck she could not catch. She began to tremble uncontrollably. Had he not been holding her, she might have fallen.

The gown slipped to her ankles. He loosened the net that held her hair, letting it tumble over her shoulders, then turned her round to face him. 'By the rood, but it's incredible!' he muttered, his eyes devouring the slim body burnished gold in the torchlight. 'What lucky chance can have brought you here tonight?'

She saw with dismay that he had already removed his mask, and involuntarily put up a hand to check that her own was still in place.

'Leave it!' he snapped peremptorily, misunderstanding her gesture. 'I don't wish to see your face.'

Giulia stared at him, bewildered. As if regretting the sharpness of his tone, he stepped towards her, his expression softening. 'Don't misunderstand me. You have a lovely face, I've no doubt. But I beg you—don't remove your mask till we have snuffed the candles, for that would spoil the illusion.'

She had only a moment to wonder at this explanation before he pulled her roughly into his arms. His mouth came down hard on hers, forcing her lips apart without waiting for her response, while his hands moved urgently over her body, holding her close against him as if to make her aware of his mounting excitement. His kiss deepened, hungrily demanding, until she felt she must surely suffocate. Desperate for air, she began to struggle, but this seemed only to increase his desire. Without raising his mouth from hers he lifted her in his arms and ascended the dais, almost falling with her on to the bed. For a brief second she was free at last to catch her breath; but in the next instant he had torn open his clothing and was upon her, taking her swiftly and ruthlessly with the frenzied passion of a man who had held himself in check too long. Against this onslaught Giulia was powerless. Too shocked even to resist his painful, unloving invasion of her body, she lay passive beneath him, conscious only that at the height of his ecstasy the name he called out was her own. 'Giulia! Oh, *Giulia* . . . !'

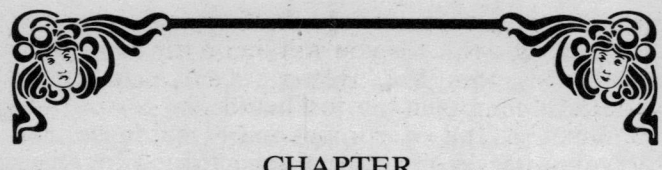

CHAPTER NINE

SHE LAY weeping silently. He moved away to lie on his back and said in the polite, detached tone of a stranger, 'I hurt you. I'm sorry. I was possessed of a demon.'

She moistened her lips. 'You—called me—by another name.' Her voice sounded hoarse and unfamiliar in her own ears. 'You called me—Giulia.'

'No!' His denial came swiftly, on a note of anguish; but in the next instant he had regained control. 'You were mistaken. I called you Ginette. The names are very similar.'

She said nothing. Perhaps it *had* been mere wishful thinking that made her imagine the cry still ringing in her ears.

He raised himself on one elbow to look down at her. 'You spoke truly when you said your husband neglected you. You've never, I think, known a man before tonight?'

Wordlessly, she shook her head. The tears ran unchecked down her cheeks, falling from beneath her mask on to the silken coverlet.

'If I'd realised . . .' He checked, then gave a sigh of bitter self-reproach. 'Well, 'tis too late now. I used you selfishly, to serve my own purpose, though heaven knows you did not deserve such treatment.'

She forced herself to speak. 'It does not matter.'

'I fear it does, for you will be on my conscience for the rest of my life.' He put out a hand to brush a strand of hair from her forehead. The gesture was tender and full of compassion. Unable to bear the remorse in his eyes, Giulia turned her back on him and pressed her burning face against the pillow.

He went on quietly, 'My only excuse is your beauty. It made me forget everything save my own need. You're exquisite, Ginette . . .' His hand moved over her shoulder and slid downwards, exploring the curve of her waist and hip. Her flesh quivered at his touch, but she was still too full of hurt to respond and lay inert beneath his caresses. She heard him give a sharp intake of breath, then he murmured close to her ear, 'Perhaps I can make amends . . .'

Before she had realised what he was doing he leant across her to snuff the candles. Then, in the anonymity of the dark, he removed her mask, casting it on to the floor, and turned her face towards his, kissing the tears first from her eyes and then her cheeks until he found her mouth. This time, however, he made no attempt to force her response but used his lips and tongue persuasively, almost teasingly, until at last her numbed senses began to stir. With considerable skill and artistry he coaxed her body alive again, playing upon it as if she were a flute and he the most practised of musicians. At last the blood began to flow once more through her veins, restoring the feeling in her nerve-ends to a tingling awareness of his touch. She sensed that although now fully aroused himself he was holding back, waiting till she was ready for him. Miraculously her tension melted away and she felt herself softening, opening like a flower beneath him.

With a murmur of satisfaction he entered her as easily and naturally as if they had been fashioned for each other. And this time there was no pain, only a piercing pleasure such as she had never imagined possible, to be followed by wave upon wave of unbelievable sensation as they moved together in perfect harmony towards the moment when all thought and emotion and feeling were united in final rapture.

And this time it was she who cried aloud, a wordless shout of pure joy and fulfilment.

They lay at peace, the tumult stilled.

'Ginette,' he murmured at length. 'You have banished my demons. No other woman can have power over me now.'

Still she could not speak, her heart too full for words.

'When I came here tonight I had not thought to find such happiness,' he went on, his lips against her throat. 'All I looked for was a temporary easing of my torment, no more. How could I know that Fate had decided to smile on me for once?'

She stroked his hair, glorying in the freedom to touch him at last without fear of rebuff, and gently kissed the beads of perspiration from his brow.

'But were you not aware of the risks you ran, coming alone to this house?' He held her closer, as if she were a child in need of his protection.

'I knew there were risks,' she admitted. 'But I could not help myself. I—I was so restless . . .'

'It seems that both our needs were great!' There was a hint of laughter in his voice, and an underlying note of exultation. 'I only hope your satisfaction may be equal to my own?'

'I think you already know the answer to that, monsieur.'

He gave a low chuckle.

Taking courage from this new-born intimacy in the dark, she said softly, 'If I pleased you, then I am glad.' Her fingers found the scars that covered his back. 'For you have not had a happy life, I think?'

For a moment he was silent and she feared she might have misjudged his mood. But then he said quite unemotionally, 'Many men returned from the Turkish wars with the scars of battle on their bodies.'

'But these were not made with the sword, I fancy?' Lightly she ran her hands over the hard ridges, knowing this time that they would not give her away by their roughness. 'Were you taken captive, monsieur, and ill-treated by the infidels?'

'I was captured, yes. But not ill treated—at least not by the Ottomans. My captor was the Sultan himself, Mehmet the Conqueror and, far from treating me ill, he made me his friend.'

'His friend?' Giulia was startled.

'I found him a wise man, a far-sighted and just ruler of his people. It seemed to me that the new society he was building in Constantinople was admirable, in many ways the very opposite of the corrupt and murderous society I had left behind in Venice.'

She remembered what the Prioress had told her: that Pietro had gone away to sea soon after the murder of his parents, when he was disenchanted with the ways of the Republic.

'I was younger then, and more impressionable,' he continued. 'When the Sultan treated me as his trusted friend and adviser, I was flattered and told him all I knew of the Venetian navy at that time and of our tactics in battle. In return he treated me more as an honoured guest than as a captive and gave me a house of my own, with servants to wait upon me. For that alone many would call me traitor.'

He was speaking without constraint. Laura Rocco's words came into her mind—'*If he wishes to talk, don't try to stop him . . .*'

So she listened without comment while he told her of his life in Constantinople, of his increased freedom to travel about the countryside escorted only by a single bodyguard given him by the Sultan, and of his subsequent capture by a fierce band of Anatolian rebels. It was they who had imprisoned him and flogged him to the point of death, until he was boldly rescued by his bodyguard, who took him to his childhood home not far away and hid him from his pursuers. 'I escaped by taking refuge in a well,' Pietro said, his voice for the first time betraying some emotion. 'But they tortured my guard, tearing out his tongue when he would not tell them where I was hiding.'

Kasim!

'And if that wasn't enough, they cruelly assaulted his sister, leaving her broken in spirit and so badly scarred that she will never show her face to any man.' His voice shook with anger. 'I have them both with me still, at my house in Venice, for I owe them my life and do what little I can to repay them for their sacrifice.'

Giulia lay quite still, feeling suddenly cold. *Zoe was Kasim's sister . . .* The tears came once more into her eyes. How little she had understood them both. Indeed, she had not even troubled to inquire into the true reason for the servant-girl's fearful, timid ways. She felt ashamed and vowed to make amends . . .

'And so I was able to return to Constantinople,' Pietro concluded, 'where the Sultan welcomed me back like a long-lost son. But my experience had unsettled me. I began to see things I could not agree with. For example, the Sultan had introduced a law decreeing that whichever of his sons seized the throne after his death should have the right to murder his brothers. Constantinople was no better than Venice. My eyes were open and I was no longer enchanted. So I begged leave to come home.'

'And the Sultan made no objection?'

'It suited his purpose. He was anxious to end the war with Venice, and sent me back to go before the Council with proposals for peace. It was then we began the negotiations that led to the final treaty.' He gave a long sigh. 'The terms were hard, yet I believe we were right to accept them. I am a sailor, but, like most Venetians, I prefer to trade rather than make war.'

'And now you are home, are you content?' Giulia asked. 'Or do you still prefer the ways of the East?'

He sighed. ''Tis true there's much about their civilisation that appeals to me strongly. But it's based on the philosophy of Islam—and I am too much a Christian ever to feel completely at ease there.'

'And did their women appeal to you strongly?' she asked provocatively. 'They say that oriental women are very beautiful.'

'So they are.' He raised his head to claim her lips again, lingeringly and possessively. 'But none can compare with you, my Ginette.'

'Yet you still haven't seen my face . . .' No sooner had she said the words than she regretted them, for in the next instant he sat up and swung his legs over the side of the bed.

'Then it's time we remedied the matter,' he said gaily, almost boyishly. 'For I no longer fear . . .'

'No!' She flung herself towards him, catching hold of his arm. 'Do not light the candle, I beg you!' She pulled herself closer, winding her arms around his neck and covering the side of his face with small, desperate kisses. 'I do not want you to leave me, even for a second.'

His hesitation was only momentary, for as her mouth found his in the darkness, the fire that had merely been slumbering between them sprang once more into life. Soon they were consumed by the flames of a passion even stronger than before, leading them on to new and increasingly pleasurable discoveries until it seemed as though they could never have their fill of each other. And when towards dawn they lay clasped in a drowsy, sensuous embrace, Pietro murmured, 'We must meet again, my love. I cannot bear to lose you now.'

With a sense of shock, Giulia realised that in the heady delight of all that had passed between them she had almost forgotten the true purpose of her mission. His arm lay heavy across her body, his hand stroking the soft skin of her thigh. She covered it with her own, touching the ring he wore on his little finger.

Turning her face towards him, she brushed her lips against his neck. 'It may not be possible for us to meet again. Soon you set sail . . . and when you return I shall be gone from Venice. Give me something, I pray you . . . Something of your own whereby I may remember you. This ring . . .'

He stiffened momentarily; then relaxed. 'The ring of approval . . . Why not? Heaven knows you deserve it, far more than . . .' He sat up, taking the ring from his finger. 'Give me your hand.'

She obeyed him; and as he put on the slim gold band she gave a little shudder of triumph. Her plan had succeeded beyond her wildest dreams.

'You're cold?' His voice was full of concern.

'No, no . . . I am warm! Come, let me show you how warm I am!' Once again he willingly allowed himself to be diverted, and when at last he fell asleep the pale light of dawn was already creeping through the window to lie across the pillows, restoring a touch of gold to the bedhead with its ornately carved foliage.

Gently Giulia eased herself away. She must leave before daylight or there would be a risk of discovery. She dressed quickly and picked up the mask from where it lay on the floor. Then, with a last look at the sleeping form of her husband spread-eagled across the bed, she silently slipped from the room.

The house was deathly quiet. Nothing stirred. She crept along the corridor, wondering where she might look for her cloak. Certainly not on this floor, for who could guess what illicit coupling was taking place behind those closed doors. But perhaps in one of the rooms downstairs . . . ?

There were no servants about to direct her. She reached the salon and hesitated, uncertain which way to go. When a figure detached itself from the shadows and came towards her, she gave a start, then saw it was Laura Rocco in a robe of dark red velvet, her golden hair hanging loose about her shoulders.

They surveyed each other for a moment without speaking. The cold grey light seeping in through the tall windows of the salon was not kind to the courtesan. It showed up the lines and wrinkles on her face, betraying that she was no longer young.

'You've done well,' she said cryptically. ''Tis a pity you're not long in Venice or I would suggest you visit my house again.'

Giulia flushed. 'I fear that will not be possible. If I could have my cloak . . .'

'I have it here, waiting for you.' She took Francesca's orange cloak from the chair and placed it round Giulia's shoulders, turning her to face the light. 'Let me look at you without your mask.'

Giulia held her breath, half-expecting to be recognised. It was true that when they had met outside the convent Laura had not appeared even to glance at her, yet surely she must have some motive for subjecting her now to such a searching scrutiny.

'I'm amazed that you are French,' the courtesan remarked. 'For your looks are most typically Venetian. Indeed, you could almost be my daughter.'

Giulia stared at her incredulously. She saw at once what Laura Rocco meant, for their colouring was identical—and surely the set of the eyes was the same above the high cheekbones . . . and the full-lipped, curving mouth.

'For your sake, however, 'tis as well you're not,' said the courtesan, suddenly brusque. 'I will summon you a gondola.'

Giulia tried to gather her wits. 'If you please—

not your own gondola, in case . . .' Her voice tailed off.

'In case your husband should question the boatman?' Laura smiled. 'I understand. You forget, I'm well versed in the art of discretion.'

'Thank you, madame.' Giulia lowered her eyes. 'I'm most grateful to you for—for allowing me to stay.'

'My dear, you've no need to thank me.' Laura's mouth twisted ironically. 'On the contrary, 'tis I who should thank *you*.'

Giving Giulia no time to query this surprising statement, she rang for a servant to escort her down to the water-gate. Then, without a word of farewell, she turned to mount the staircase, the hem of her velvet robe sweeping over the marble steps.

The Grand Canal was already busy with traffic at this early hour, mostly tradesmen plying their barges laden with fruit and vegetables and fish on their way to market. Though none of them spared her gondola more than a passing glance, Giulia retreated behind the curtains of the cabin, taking advantage of this brief respite to gather her troubled thoughts.

Her mind was full of Laura Rocco's strange remarks. Could the courtesan be her mother? She found the thought disturbing, for although there was undoubtedly a strong physical resemblance between them, Laura Rocco was far from being the kind of mother she had liked to imagine. She was too cold, too calculating . . . and yet this morning she had looked upon her almost kindly, as if she approved of her. But for what reason Giulia could not guess—unless it was because she had proved herself the true daughter of a courtesan, who could keep a man so enslaved by her charms that he would stay with her till morning?

A hot tide of embarrassment swept over her. How often had Pietro accused her of being a whore? And surely last night she had proved him right, giving herself to him without stint or shame in ways no virtuous woman would countenance for an instant. Wasn't this in itself sufficient proof that she must be the daughter of Laura Rocco—and therefore hardly a fitting wife for a nobleman of Venice?

She stared down at the ring on her finger, twisting it round and round as if to assure herself it was not a figment of her imagination. When Pietro came home she must show it to him at once, or it would be too late to stop the annulment before he set sail for the Levant.

But how she dreaded that moment when she revealed the true identity of Ginette de Narbonne! Would he be amused to discover how he had been tricked . . . or so furiously angry that he would never forgive her?

For the answer, she must wait until his return.

The Ca' Gabrieli was barely astir when she arrived at the water-gate. A footman greeted her on the stairs with a slightly puzzled expression as if uncertain who she was—and no wonder, since few of the servants had set eyes on her since the wedding.

When she reached her bedchamber there was no sign of Kasim. She entered and called for Zoe, but the servant-girl too seemed to have disappeared. Perhaps they had gone in search of her, hoping to find her before Pietro learned she was missing? She felt a stab of guilt, realising she had placed both brother and sister in a difficult position. Now that she knew their true story, she could no longer resent them for obeying their master's orders.

With some difficulty she managed to take off Francesca's gown, blushing as she recalled how speedily Pietro had performed the same task last night; and when she was clothed once more in oriental robe and caftan she settled down on the divan, composing herself as best she could to await his return. For a while she tried to read the book that had served her so well, but found it impossible to concentrate. Her eyelids felt heavy as lead and she had a struggle to keep awake. Last night she had slept even less than Pietro, fearing to relax her guard for an instant, and now sheer physical exhaustion was fast overtaking her. Eventually her head dropped back against the cushions and she fell into a deep, dreamless sleep.

It was past noon when she awoke with a start. Some sort of commotion seemed to be taking place outside in the corridor. There were sounds of a struggle and raised voices, culminating in a high-pitched childish scream. She crossed the room and flung open her door.

At the far end of the corridor Monna Clarissa was engaged in an undignified tug-of-war with a tearful, white-faced Gentile, who resisted strongly her attempts to drag him down the stairs. Watching them was Cardinal Lorenzo Benetti, his saturnine face as impassive as ever, while her husband's steward hovered close by, plainly undecided whether or not he should intervene.

'Stop!' Giulia moved swiftly towards them. 'What are you doing with Gentile?'

Monna Clarissa, taken by surprise, momentarily

relaxed her grip on the boy's arm. He immediately threw himself at Giulia, catching hold of the rich material of her caftan.

'We're removing him,' said the Cardinal, 'from this house of degradation.'

'Why? Because he has dared at last to show a little spirit?' Giulia placed a reassuring arm around Gentile's shoulders and looked from one to the other of them, thinking they were the most inhuman pair she had ever encountered. Monna Clarissa's face was contorted with spite, whereas the Cardinal's hooded eyes burned with a fiercely determined light.

'My aunt informs me that recently he's been impossible to handle. Twice he's disobeyed her orders.'

'If you're referring to the time he came to find me in my room, then surely you're being unreasonable? We played a game together—Is that so dreadful a crime?'

'It shows a regrettable want of discipline!' spat Monna Clarissa.

'A child of six cannot be ruled by discipline alone! He needs love and understanding and—and *laughter*.' Giulia gazed helplessly at their harsh, implacable faces. 'I can give him all these things if you allow him to stay.'

''Tis far too late for that,' the Cardinal said coldly. 'I've made up my mind that from now on he must be brought up where he belongs, as a member of the Benetti household.'

'But you've no right! His father . . .'

'His father no longer has any say in the matter.' He held out his white, long-fingered hand with its glittering onyx ring. 'Come, Gentile.'

The child pressed himself even closer to Giulia.

She stroked his hair comfortingly. 'I insist you wait till my husband returns. He won't be long . . .'

The Cardinal uttered a short, mirthless laugh. 'On the contrary, I think that Pietro Gabrieli will not be returning to this house for some considerable time.'

She stared at him, paling. 'What do you mean?'

'I mean that his base, immoral nature has at last betrayed him. By his own behaviour he has forfeited the right to bring up my nephew in his house.' The Cardinal's contemptuous gaze slid over her caftan, her pale face and disordered hair. 'And you, madonna, are plainly no better than he! Come, give me the child.'

Stunned by his accusation, Giulia offered no resistance as Gentile was dragged away from her. Holding his screaming nephew in a steely grip, the Cardinal set off down the stairs, followed by an agitated but triumphant Monna Clarissa.

Giulia stood still, holding a hand to her heart. Her eyes met those of the steward, whose face was as shocked as her own.

'Where is my husband?' she demanded.

'I—I don't know, madonna.'

'And Kasim . . . and Zoe—where are they?'

He spread his hands wide in a helpless gesture. 'They appear to have gone.'

'But is there *no one* . . .?' She broke off, biting her lip and thinking hard. Alessandro! 'Where is my husband's brother?'

'He, too, is missing, madonna. He left the house at first light and hasn't yet returned.'

She was gripped by a sudden panic. Was she completely alone at the Ca' Gabrieli? Fearing to betray herself in front of the steward, she ran back into her room and closed the door. Once inside she tried to calm her whirling thoughts, telling herself that the Cardinal must have been bluffing. He could not possibly be certain that Pietro would not be coming home.

Unless he knew something that she did not . . . ?'

She pressed her hands to her burning cheeks and began pacing restlessly up and down. If only Pietro would hurry back so that she could tell him about Gentile! Her own confession now seemed unimportant. She longed only to see him again, to reassure herself that he was safe . . .

At a knock on her door she swung round expectantly. But it was Francesca who entered, her face wreathed in smiles. 'My dear, I *had* to come and find out how last night . . .'

'Oh, Francesca—I'm so glad to see you!' Giulia seized her by the arm and pulled her urgently into the room. 'I don't know what's happening. Everyone has gone . . . Kasim and Zoe—and now Gentile. I'm half out of my mind with worry.'

Francesca looked at her, concerned. 'What do you mean—Gentile has gone?'

She listened gravely while Giulia recounted how Gentile had been snatched from the house by his uncle. 'The Cardinal is a bigot,' Francesca declared. 'He sees evil everywhere and is far too quick to condemn. But you may depend upon it that Pietro will act immediately he comes home. He will never allow his son to be brought up as a Benetti.'

'But if he doesn't come home *soon*, he won't know!' Giulia said despairingly. 'He must have gone straight to the Arsenal. Oh, Francesca—I'd staked everything on seeing him at least once more before he sails . . . but now it seems I was mistaken. He doesn't even care enough to bid me farewell.'

Francesca's gaze alighted on Giulia's tightly clasped hands. 'I see you're wearing his ring,' she said, leaving the question in her eyes unstated.

Giulia nodded unhappily. 'Yes . . . he has given me his ring.'

'Then surely you've every reason to expect he'll come to bid you farewell?'

'He—he did not guess my true identity.' She raised pleading eyes to Francesca's face. 'Please, will you come with me to the Arsenal? If we hurry, we may catch him before he sails.'

Francesca looked taken aback, but she quickly recovered. 'Yes, of course I'll come with you. But you'd best put on the cloak I lent you last night. 'Twill make you less conspicuous than that Turkish robe.'

Giulia hesitated, then remembered that Pietro had not seen the cloak, for she had discarded it on entering Laura Rocco's salon. She swung it round her shoulders and together they went downstairs to Francesca's waiting gondola.

At the Arsenal the day's work was not yet ended. The yards were still full of the hammering and shouting of men at work on the new State galleys, and the smell of boiling pitch rose up to mingle with the salty air. For here they were close to the sea, at the very extremity of the city, and within the harbour's sheltering arm lay the merchant fleet of Venice, making ready to sail.

Francesca ordered her boatman to enquire which was her brother's ship, and on being told it was *The Golden Lion* they found it without difficulty, for it was the largest and finest vessel in sight. All cargo was now aboard and the sailors were carrying out their final tasks. They glanced at the two women with some curiosity, but as Giulia was about to ask one of them the whereabouts of his captain, Francesca gripped her arm. 'Look who is here!' she exclaimed.

Giulia followed her pointing finger. Leaning carelessly against a bollard on the quayside was the slender, dandyish figure of Alessandro. He turned at once when they called, and came towards them.

'Francesca! And my fair sister-in-law . . . this is indeed an honour! Have you come to wish me *bon voyage*?'

'We hadn't even realised you were sailing,' Francesca said, showing her astonishment.

''Twas not my intention,' he admitted, then added with an air of bravado. 'However, it seemed no less than my duty to step into the breach.'

'What breach is this?' inquired his sister.

Alessandro drew himself up to his full height. 'I've offered myself to take command in my brother's absence.'

'In his *absence*?' Giulia repeated, bewildered. 'But why? Where *is* Pietro?'

'Have you not heard?' Alessandro looked surprised. 'But I had assumed he was at home when the order came, and he was taken from the Ca' Gabrieli.'

Giulia stared at him, all colour ebbing from her face.

'What do you mean—*taken*?' Francesca demanded. 'Stop talking in riddles, Brother, and tell us at once what has happened to Pietro.'

'Why, he's been arrested . . . and is being held on a charge of treason against the State!' He looked hard at Giulia as he spoke. 'I fear the punishment may be death.'

CHAPTER TEN

THE GONDOLA carried them swiftly back to the city. Within its curtained cabin Giulia and Francesca sat in appalled silence.

'He must have known,' Giulia murmured at last. 'The Cardinal must have known what had happened or he wouldn't have dared to take Gentile.'

'No doubt he'd heard the news from someone in the Council,' Francesca agreed.

'But I don't understand why they should arrest Pietro *now*, after all this time. Surely, if they wanted to accuse him of treason, it would have been more reasonable to do so immediately after his return from Constantinople?'

'He was then engaged in negotiating the Peace . . .'

'And doesn't *that* in itself proclaim his innocence?'

Francesca said uneasily, 'Most people consider that the terms of the treaty favour the Turks far more than ourselves.' When Giulia made no comment, she went on, 'Pietro has his enemies, my dear. Indeed, what man of substance in Venice does not? I don't doubt there's someone who's only been awaiting the chance to denounce him.'

'Such as the Cardinal . . . or Alessandro?'

'Oh, my dear, no!' Francesca sounded genuinely shocked. 'I can't believe Alessandro capable of such an act. Indeed, he's doing his best to save the family honour by taking command of Pietro's ship, for he's a poor sailor and suffers dreadfully when the weather is rough.'

Giulia bit her lip, unwilling to offend her sister-in-law. But secretly she thought that if it *was* Alessandro who had betrayed his brother, would this not merely be a case of history repeating itself? And as for his noble gesture in taking Pietro's place, this could easily have been prompted by a desire to leave Venice as soon as possible—a desire so strong as to overcome his natural dislike of the sea.

'. . . you will have much to do,' Francesca was saying. 'In the absence of both my brothers, you must take upon yourself the running of the household. Naturally I shall help you all I can.'

'My first task is to secure Pietro's release,' Giulia said abruptly. 'Nothing else matters till that is achieved.'

Francesca stared at her. 'But how will you do that?'

'I shall appeal to the Grand Council. Surely they're not so inhuman as to refuse me an audience?'

Francesca looked doubtful. 'You'll need help. Someone in a position of authority.'

'Your husband?' Giulia suggested. 'Could he not be persuaded to petition on my behalf?'

'Alas, he's far too old and feeble in his wits. No one listens to him now,' Francesca said frankly. 'Why don't you send word to your father? He isn't a Venetian, 'tis true, but he's a wealthy man and may be able to wield some influence.'

Giulia shook her head, thinking that Ercole Tebaldi would be of little use in such an emergency.

He was far too anxious to avoid trouble at all costs. Indeed, there seemed to be no one she could turn to for help. She had no friends in Venice, let alone someone who had the ear of the Council.

Except . . .

She turned to Francesca. 'Will you tell your boatman to take me to the Convent of S. Cecilia. I'll talk to the Prioress. Pietro himself told me that many important men in Venice go to her for counsel.'

Francesca looked dubious. 'For spiritual counsel, perhaps . . . but this is hardly a spiritual matter.'

Giulia said obstinately, 'I believe that, if anyone can help me, 'tis the Prioress.'

'Very well.' With a shrug Francesca leaned forward to address her boatman. He changed direction at once, and a short while later drew in beside the steps leading up to the convent's water-gate.

'Don't wait for me,' Giulia told her sister-in-law. 'I shall be some time.'

'Would you like me to come in with you?'

She shook her head. 'I'd prefer to see her alone.'

Only with the Prioress could she be herself, Giulia thought as she watched Francesca's gondola pull away from the steps. It would be a welcome relief to speak honestly to someone who knew the whole story. Moreover, Mother Maria had already shown compassion in the matter of Caterina; surely she would lend an equally sympathetic ear to Giulia's own problems?

She mounted the steps and rang the bell.

The Prioress received her in her office. She bade Giulia be seated and herself took a chair on the other side of the desk. 'No doubt you're anxious about Caterina,' she said. 'I'm glad to tell you she's much improved, though still not strong enough to leave her bed for more than a few hours each day. However, she has a constant visitor who seems to do her considerably more good than any physician. I think I need not tell you his name?'

Giulia shook her head. 'You've been most kind.'

'Kind?' The Prioress raised an eyebrow. ' 'Tis not so much a question of kindness as of commonsense. Caterina has neither the physical nor mental stamina required for the solitary life. She would not last above a twelvemonth. That's why I've arranged for her to marry her Bernardo as soon as she's fit to do so.'

'That's wonderful news.' Giulia tried to sound enthusiastic.

'But perhaps Caterina was not after all the main purpose of your visit,' the Prioress said shrewdly. ' 'Tis plain you've something else on your mind.'

The nun's calm, matter-of-fact manner gave Giulia the confidence she needed. Quietly and succinctly she recounted all that happened since the Cardinal came to snatch Gentile, for this had been the first moment when she suspected something was wrong. What she did *not* relate, however, were the events of the previous night. This was partly because she was reluctant to confess her visit to the house of Laura Rocco for fear of offending the nun's sensibilities, but also because it seemed to her irrelevant. What had passed between herself and Pietro was private and had nothing to do with the present situation.

The Prioress listened attentively; and when Giulia had finished, she rose from her chair to pull the bell-rope. When a lay sister appeared, she asked for writing-paper and a quill.

'You need more information,' she said, returning to her seat. 'I'll give you a letter to take to Procurator Martinelli. He should be able to find out for you on what grounds these charges have been made and by whom your husband is accused.'

Giulia reflected that Pietro had spoken truly in saying that the Prioress had friends in high places. A Procurator was one of the highest Venetian dignitaries, higher even than a Senator.

When the lay sister returned, the Prioress set about composing her letter, covering the paper quickly with bold, spidery handwriting. At last she penned her signature, applied a seal and handed the letter across the desk to Giulia. 'The Procurator lives but a short walk from here. I shall send a Sister to escort you.' When Giulia tried to express her thanks, she added warningly, 'Don't expect miracles. I fear 'tis not within his power to effect your husband's release. None the less he should be able to furnish you with the information you require. Then we can decide upon the next step to be taken.'

Giulia's eyes filled with tears of gratitude. Impulsively she sank on to her knees and pressed her lips to Mother Maria's ring.

The nun's other hand rested fleetingly upon her head. 'Go in peace, my child.'

Procurator Martinelli was a stout, middle-aged man of florid complexion, but his blue eyes were sharply alive, suggesting that his brain was a good deal more agile than his rather ponderous body. He wore the red damask toga that proclaimed his rank, and received Giulia in a palatial chamber decorated with frescoes.

More than a little in awe of him, she curtsied low and handed over the letter without saying a word.

He took it from her and scanned it twice, glancing up from time to time to look into her face.

At length he said abruptly, 'Do you know the contents of my sister's letter?'

Giulia was taken aback. She had not for an instant suspected that Procurator Martinelli was related to the Prioress.

'I—I have not read it, my lord,' she stammered. 'But I'm aware the Prioress has requested your help on my behalf.'

He stared at her a moment longer before saying, 'Your husband is Pietro Gabrieli. I knew his father well. He was a fine man.'

Giulia raised her chin. 'My husband is also a fine man—and innocent, I'm certain, of the charges brought against him.'

The Procurator frowned. 'You know of his involvement with the Sultan Mehmet?'

'Why, yes . . . but all that's in the past. He owes the Sultan no further loyalty, he told me so himself.'

His gaze rested thoughtfully on her troubled face. 'There are those, I fear, who find that difficult to believe. However . . .' He stopped, then gave a small, decisive nod. 'Wait here.'

Left alone, Giulia occupied herself by taking stock of her surroundings. She found it strange to think the Prioress had once lived in this house, and couldn't help wondering what made a woman born into such wealth and luxury give up everything to become a nun. A strong sense of vocation, she supposed, and a dislike of worldly values.

It was over an hour before Procurator Martinelli returned. 'I fear I've learned little more than was contained in my sister's letter,' he said apologetically. 'As we knew, the charge is treason—on the grounds that he conspired with the Turkish Sultan against the Republic. But his accuser is anonymous.'

'Anonymous?'

'Someone who has used the lion's mouth.'

Giulia turned pale. She had heard of the letter-boxes in the shape of a lion's head wherein any citizen of Venice might secretly place his accusation against another. The custom had helped to gain the Republic its sinister reputation as a hotbed of spies.

But who could have written that fatal letter?

As though he had picked up her thoughts, the Procurator asked, 'Have you any idea who your husband's enemy might be?'

She hesitated, reluctant to put her suspicions into words. 'I know of at least two people who stand to gain by his removal. But surely the Council cannot condemn him merely on hearsay, without evidence of any kind?'

'Indeed no. Whoever made this accusation must have done so knowing that their case would stand up in a court of law. This means, of course, that there are witnesses.'

'Witnesses?' She stared at him, startled. 'But who . . . ?'

'That I was unable to discover. 'Tis more than likely their names will not be put forward till just before the trial.'

'And when will that be?'

'It may take several weeks before the case against him is prepared. In the meantime, I fear, he must languish in gaol.'

She stood up. 'Then may I see him, please?'

The Procurator gave her an odd look. 'During the course of my inquiries I came across another matter. Are you aware that your husband recently filed a petition for the annulment of your marriage?'

For a moment she was unable to speak. Pietro's arrest had totally driven the annulment from her mind. At last she said in a low voice, 'Yes, I knew of it. But matters between us have changed since then. I—I'm hoping he will withdraw the petition.'

A gleam of sympathy showed in Procurator Martinelli's sharp blue eyes. 'I hope so, too, for it seems to me you're a young woman of character. Pietro Gabrieli should count himself lucky.'

She flushed. 'A woman of character' was exactly how Ercole had described her mother. Was this a quality she had inherited from Laura Rocco?

'However, I think we may safely assume the annulment will be left in abeyance until after the trial,' the Procurator continued. 'By which time any difference between you and your husband may have been resolved. Now, do you still wish to see him?'

She nodded dumbly.

The Ducal Palace was far more than merely the private residence of the rulers of Venice. Behind its pink-and-white façade lay council chambers, courts, a torture-chamber and two prisons—one for petty thieves and ruffians, the other for those accused of crimes against the State. It was in the latter, known as the Leads from its situation high up beneath the roof, that Pietro was being held. Not the most fragrant of places, the Procurator warned Giulia as the door was opened to them by a surly, long-faced gaoler.

As if to prove his point, a stench of rotting straw and human excrement came drifting along the dark corridor that led to the cells. They were shown into a low-ceilinged room with bars at the window and told to wait until the prisoner was brought to them.

Giulia felt suddenly nervous. Try as she would to suppress it, the memory of last night was still vivid in her mind. Beneath her glove she could feel the hard ridge of Pietro's ring . . . but how to tell him? She wished now she had prepared a speech.

In fact his appearance, when he was finally thrust into the room, drove all other thoughts from her mind. He wore his own cambric shirt open to the waist, his hair was unkempt and his chin unshaven. But it was his eyes that shocked her most. They were dull, almost glazed, regarding her with no pleasure or even curiosity, only a weary apathy.

Giulia turned to the gaoler. 'May I speak to my husband alone, please?'

He glanced at Procurator Martinelli, who gave him a brief nod. 'Five minutes,' he said curtly.

'I'll wait outside the door,' said the Procurator, adding in a low tone, 'Be warned—you'd best not pass him anything to aid his escape. It will only make matters worse than they already are.'

'I have nothing,' Giulia assured him, spreading out her gloved hands.

The two men left the room, closing the door behind them.

Giulia looked at her husband. He was gazing fixedly at the barred window as if unaware of her presence. She gripped the back of a chair for support but felt no wish to sit down, even though her legs were trembling. She was all too aware that she had only five minutes . . . and that Pietro seemed far away from her, in another world.

'My lord?' she began tentatively.

He turned to her with a look of mild surprise. 'Why have you come?'

'I want to help you.'

'I'm afraid that's impossible.'

'No!' Her fingers tightened on the chair-back. 'You must not lose hope. Surely there's *something* we can do?'

He shook his head. 'I'm accused of treason. They will try me and find me guilty. That's all there is to it.'

'But don't you mean to defend yourself?'

'What's the use?' he said with a shrug.

'For pity's sake, have they managed to break your spirit so soon?' She felt a rising impatience. 'You *must* fight back—for Gentile's sake if not your own.'

'Gentile?' At last she had caught his attention.

'The Cardinal has taken him from the Ca' Gabrieli,' Giulia explained. 'I tried to prevent him, but he was adamant. Indeed, he must already have known of your arrest.'

Pietro frowned. 'This is what he's been waiting for, of course—The chance to denounce me as unfit to bring up my own son.'

'Then you must prove yourself innocent of the charge brought against you!' She gazed at him imploringly. 'My lord, we've so little time. Have you *no* idea who your accuser may be?'

'Oh, yes,' he said calmly. 'I know who she is.'

'*She?*' Giulia was taken aback.

'Ah, that surprises you?' His expression was cynical. 'Well, it's no use my trying to dissemble, for I fear it will all come out at my trial. The truth is that I spent last night with a most desirable young Frenchwoman—so desirable, indeed, that I quite lost my head.'

Giulia stared at him, dumbstruck.

Taking her silence for reproach, he went on,

'You've no reason to look at me like that, Giulia. Indeed, the blame is partly yours, since it was her likeness to you that first attracted me.'

She made some effort to recover her wits. 'What—what was her name?'

'Ginette.' He smiled ironically. 'Even that, you see, is similar to your own. Ginette de Narbonne. The odd thing is that she proved to be a virgin. A clever ruse . . .'

'A ruse?'

'Of course. It served to deprive me of my natural caution. I was so thrown off my guard by this astonishing discovery that I believed her to be exactly what she seemed—a sweetly innocent creature neglected by her ageing husband.'

Giulia moistened her dry lips. 'But now you don't believe she *is* . . . innocent?'

'Far from it.' His tone was bitter. 'Oh, she was clever—diabolically so. In the aftermath of love I became weak as putty in her hands. Without appearing to do so, she encouraged me to talk. Indeed, I confided in her things I have never told another living soul.'

'What—manner of things?'

'The truth of my captivity in Turkey, of how well I was treated, and of the help I gave the Sultan in return. More than enough to condemn me in the eyes of my countrymen.'

Giulia's brain was reeling. She remembered all too well their conversation within the dark seclusion of the courtesan's bed . . . but no one else could possibly have heard it. How could they?

She murmured weakly, 'Surely you must be mistaken . . .'

'I fear not. In fact she gave herself away, though I was far too bewitched at the time to realise it.

Towards the end of our night together she asked me for a keepsake, something to remind her of me.'

Guiltily Giulia thrust her hand behind her back lest he should see the outline of his ring inside her glove.

'We should not meet again, she said, before I set sail.' His mouth set in a bitter line. 'How could she have known I was about to leave Venice? *I* had not mentioned it to her.'

'You might have let it slip,' Giulia said wildly, cursing herself for being so careless. 'You said you talked of many things . . .'

He continued as if he had not heard her. 'When I awoke, she was gone. Stolen away like a thief in the night.' His voice hardened. 'And on my way to the Arsenal, I was arrested.'

'But surely . . . ?'

He swung round, his face suddenly dark with anguish. 'I can't imagine why you're so anxious to defend her, for I must tell you honestly that in one short night she took possession of my heart and soul. In truth I fell so deeply in love with her I doubt if I shall ever again be capable of passion for another woman.' He looked at Giulia almost sorrowfully. 'In other words, my dear, she's robbed you of your power over me.'

Giulia clenched her hands behind her back. This was surely the moment when she should make her confession—yet how could she, when he held the unknown Frenchwoman responsible for his arrest?

He turned away from her, adding flatly. 'Of course she was only carrying out another's orders, though whose I neither know nor care.'

She saw that once again he was lost in his own private thoughts. He seemed obsessed by Ginette de Narbonne, convinced that she was his enemy, yet unable to shake off the fascination she held for him. Giulia found herself disliking the Frenchwoman almost as though she were her own rival.

In an attempt to break the spell, she demanded, 'Are you aware, my lord, that Alessandro has taken command of your ship?'

'If you're worrying about your father's consignment, there's no need. It's already in hand and will be taken on board, no matter who's in command.'

'It hadn't even entered my head. What I'm trying to say,' she persisted, 'is that it seems odd that Alessandro should choose to leave Venice *now*, when you've just been taken into prison.'

'It is a little surprising,' he agreed. 'One might have expected him to take advantage of my absence by making love to my wife, since that would undoubtedly give much pleasure to you both.'

Giulia flushed angrily. 'That's unfair! I've never encouraged Alessandro.'

'You had no need.' His gaze rested on her lovely face with its wide brown eyes and parted lips. For an instant a spark of interest stirred in his eyes, only to die again. He sighed. 'You've the sort of looks that can drive a man nearly out of his mind with desire, as I discovered to my cost. Well, now I'm removed from temptation and you're free to take what lovers you please. Indeed, you could do a good deal worse than Alessandro. When he returns . . .'

'Stop!' She pressed her hands to her ears. 'You mistake my meaning entirely. What I'm suggesting is that *he* may be your accuser.'

'Alessandro?' He sounded frankly incredulous. 'No, that's a preposterous notion. You're talking wildly . . .'

'*I'm trying to help you!*' In her desperation

she spoke more fiercely than she intended. She moderated her tone. 'If not Alessandro, then the Cardinal . . .'

'. . . is far too high-minded to dabble in politics.' He gave her a pitying look. 'You're out of your depth, my dear. If you'll take my advice, you'll return home to Verona at once and throw yourself on your father's mercy. I see no future for you here in Venice.'

'No!' The cry was wrung from her heart, and at that moment Procurator Martinelli came back into the room, followed by the gaoler. She appealed to them urgently. 'A few more minutes, I beg you . . .'

But Pietro had already turned to the door. 'You may return me to my cell, gaoler. This lady and I have finished with each other.'

Outside the palace Procurator Martinelli glanced at Giulia's stricken face. 'The meeting did not go as you'd hoped?'

'He will not fight,' she said despairingly. 'He will not even *try* to defend himself against the accusation. 'Tis as if he no longer cares what happens to him.'

'But *you* care, do you not?'

She nodded dully, unable to forget the ominous ring of Pietro's final words: *'This lady and I have finished with each other.'*

'I don't understand.' A frown creased the Prioress's patrician brow. 'Why are you so sure your husband's mistaken in thinking this Frenchwoman betrayed him?'

Giulia had no choice but to tell the whole story. Mother Maria listened gravely, without comment.

'I didn't mention it before,' Giulia concluded,

'because I thought it was irrelevant. Also I was afraid you might disapprove of what I had done.'

'Why should I disapprove?' the Prioress inquired. 'It seems to me you had two alternatives—either to accept the annulment or to fight back. From what I know of your character, Giulia, it doesn't surprise me in the least that you chose to fight back.'

'I should have known you'd understand,' Giulia said gratefully. 'But now you can see why I'm so mystified, since *I* am the only person in whom Pietro confided these things.'

The Prioress said slowly, 'There is *one* explanation . . . Your conversation with Pietro could have been overheard.'

'But that's impossible! We were alone together.'

'Such incidents are all too common in Venice, I fear. Secret letter-boxes, spy-holes in the ceiling, a listening device hidden in the wall . . .'

With a shock Giulia remembered the ornately carved bedhead that could so easily have concealed a cavity. 'You mean someone might have been hiding in the next room?'

Mother Maria nodded. 'At least two witnesses would be essential for this accusation to be treated seriously by the Council.'

'But that's horrible!' Giulia blushed as the full implication dawned on her, that someone had overheard everything that passed between Pietro and herself, their most intimate moments . . .

'It must have been planned in advance,' the Prioress went on. 'Laura Rocco contrived to meet your husband as if by chance and invited him to her house . . .'

'But she couldn't possibly have known that *I* would also go there!'

'That was a piece of unexpected good fortune as far as she was concerned. As soon as she saw that Pietro was attracted to the Frenchwoman, she quickly adapted her plans . . .'

'And *that*'s why she was so pleased with me next morning! She said I had done well . . .' Tears of anger started to Giulia's eyes. 'Oh, what a fool I've been! I played straight into her hands.'

'You mustn't reproach yourself. 'Tis well known that Laura Rocco's house is used for political as well as amorous intrigues. Like many of her kind, she's attracted to power.'

Giulia realised that once again she had underestimated the Prioress. Mother Maria had a far greater knowledge of what went on in the outside world than one might have expected.

'Power,' repeated the nun, 'and money. Doubtless she was well rewarded for her services last night. The question is, by whom?'

'There's only one way to find out,' Giulia said slowly. 'I shall ask her.'

'Now that *would* be foolish!' said the Prioress, alarmed. 'You're no match for Laura Rocco, child. The woman's totally ruthless.'

Giulia rose to her feet, her face pale but determined. 'Perhaps we may be better matched than you think. You see, I've reason to believe she's my mother.'

She paused only long enough to see a look of stunned amazement on the Prioress's face before she left the room.

CHAPTER ELEVEN

THE HOUR was already late when Giulia left the convent. None the less she was resolved to confront Laura Rocco straight away, while her anger was still strong enough to give her courage. Besides, she could not rest till she knew the truth.

She donned her mask and made her way on foot to the Riva degli Schiavoni, knowing that there she would have a better chance of finding a gondola at this busy time of night. The Piazzetta was crowded with revellers. Seeing her alone, some took her for a courtesan and called out ribald remarks, but she was too intent on her mission to be troubled by them. While passing the Ducal Palace, however, she had an odd conviction she was being followed, and glanced over her shoulder to see a large and familiar figure lurking beneath the arches of the colonnade.

Kasim . . .

She gave a cry and started towards him, but he immediately took flight amidst the crowds strolling through the *broglio*. Giulia gazed after him helplessly. What was he doing here, so close to where his master was imprisoned? Was he perhaps hoping to rescue Pietro as he had rescued him once before from the Anatolian rebels? If so, she feared he would find the palace guards a far more formidable obstacle. Reluctantly she turned away, wishing with all her heart that she had managed to speak to him.

To her relief she had no difficulty in finding a gondola, and on the journey tried to plan what she would say to Laura Rocco. To some extent she had no choice: since she was again wearing Francesca's distinctive cloak of burnt orange, she must play the part she had played on the previous night, of Ginette de Narbonne.

Laura Rocco received her in a private chamber. 'So, madame,' she said with a knowing smile. 'You've returned already. Am I to assume that last night's adventure proved so enjoyable that you cannot wait to repeat it?'

Giulia blushed beneath her mask.

'If so,' Laura continued, 'then I'm delighted—but I should warn you that I may not be able to provide quite such an excellent diversion again. Last night you were . . . shall we say, unusually fortunate?'

Giulia stared at the courtesan, uncertain how to begin. Laura wore a low-cut gown of silver brocade that set off her cold beauty to perfection. She was again unmasked, and her hard eyes held a speculative gleam. Totally ruthless, the Prioress had called her. Such a woman must be met on her own terms—and with weapons she would respect.

'I fear you mistake the reason for my visit, madame,' Giulia said coolly, once more assuming a French accent. 'I have no wish to take part in further adventures—at least, not unless I am assured of some recompense for my trouble.'

'Ah!' An appreciative smile flickered across the courtesan's face. 'So you're not so ingenuous as you look! I must confess I could not quite believe in the neglectful husband.' She motioned Giulia to a couch. 'Come then, let's to business.'

Giulia sat down. She waited until Laura had joined her before beginning boldly, 'Last night you said I had done well. Indeed, I carried out your instructions to the best of my ability . . .'

'My instructions?'

'To . . . make the gentleman talk.'

'Did I say that?' Laura's tone was guarded.

'You certainly implied it was what you wished me to do,' Giulia said firmly. 'I trust you learned all you wanted to know?'

Laura regarded her for a long moment without speaking. Then she said abruptly, 'May I ask you to remove your mask? In this kind of conversation I prefer to see my adversary's face.'

Adversary? She made it sound like a duel. Giulia took off her mask.

'Yes, you're a very beautiful girl,' Laura said dispassionately. 'And—as I observed before—in looks typically a Venetian. In guile too, perhaps. Tell me, why did you make no mention of this matter before you left my house this morning?'

'It had not occurred to me then. Perhaps I was, as you say, a little ingenuous. It wasn't until later, when I came to think over what had happened, that I realised you must have arranged for someone to overhear our conversation.'

The courtesan sat perfectly still, her expression wary.

Giulia saw she had the advantage. 'And I've come to the conclusion,' she went on with apparent artlessness, 'that what you wanted to know had something to do with the Turkish Sultan. You hoped the gentleman might confess . . .'

'Be quiet!' Laura interrupted, suddenly agitated.

'You should know better than to speak of such things aloud.'

Giulia bit her lip. So even here they were in danger of being overheard. Most likely every room in the house was equipped with some device for spying.

'You'd better tell me exactly what it is you want,' Laura said icily.

'I'd have thought that was obvious.' Giulia opened her eyes wide. 'Surely I've earned some payment for my services?'

'I do not submit to blackmail!' The courtesan's eyes were almost black with anger. 'Besides, I know nothing of what you speak. It has naught to do with me.'

'The incident took place in your house,' Giulia reminded her. 'Though I realise of course you were merely carrying out someone else's orders. All I ask is that you tell me who that "someone" is, so that I may apply to him directly for my reward.'

'Are you mad?' Laura leapt to her feet. 'You had best leave this instant.'

'Not until you tell me his name.' Giulia's eyes were hard and determined as the courtesan's own. 'I demand to know it! You owe me that at least.'

'*Owe* you?' Laura's voice with full of contempt. 'I owe you nothing!'

'I think you do, madonna.' Giulia gripped her hands tightly together. 'Indeed, far more than you know.'

The courtesan stared at her. 'What has become of your accent? Was that as false as your mask of innocence?'

Giulia stood up. 'Ay, for, as you rightly guessed, I am a Venetian. A true daughter of Venice, raised in the foundling hospital.' She watched Laura

Rocco's face as she spoke, hoping to see at least a momentary start of surprise, but that coldly beautiful countenance betrayed no emotion. 'Raised, that is, till the age of seven, when I was taken by my father to live at his home in Verona.'

'A touching tale, I grant you. But I fail to see . . .'

'My father's name is Ercole Tebaldi. Does *that* mean nothing to you?'

'I fear not.' Laura's eyes narrowed. 'Come, let us have done with guessing games. Tell me plainly what it is you're trying to say.'

Giulia raised her chin. 'That I'm your daughter, madonna.'

A look of total incredulity came over the courtesan's face. 'My *daughter*?'

'You yourself remarked on the likeness between us,' Giulia said, her heart pounding like a drum, now that she had delivered her ultimate weapon. 'And I know nothing of my mother save that she was a—a woman of Venice whom my father loved . . .'

'And is this your only evidence for our supposed relationship?' Laura smiled. 'Well, I shall tell you honestly that I did once bear a child . . . but it was a boy, so weak and sickly that he did not survive beyond the age of eight months. So you cannot possibly be my daughter—and if you'd hoped to have some hold over me on that score, then I fear you'll be disappointed!' She moved to the door. 'I think our interview is at an end. We've said all we need say to each other.'

'No!' Giulia's voice was sharp with desperation. 'I refuse to leave until you tell me who was the man . . . the listener in the next room.'

'Why are you so anxious to know his name?'

'I told you—that I may ask him for some recompense.'

'Then you're far better left in ignorance, for such a request would gain you nothing but an untimely death in some narrow *calle*.' Laura opened the door, giving Giulia a malicious little smile. 'You've a lot to learn, my dear. However, your looks are an undoubted asset, and if one day you should return in a less demanding frame of mind perhaps we can do business. In the meantime I must ask you to leave my house.'

Giulia saw that she was defeated. She put on her mask and drew the hood of her cloak over her head. At the door she hesitated, looking the courtesan full in the face. 'I'm glad you're not my mother,' she said in a flat, unemotional tone. 'For in truth I cannot like you very much.'

As she swept out of the room she heard Laura Rocco's low, mocking laugh behind her. A wave of cold fury broke over her, turning her limbs to ice. She descended the stairs in a trice, her brain too numbed even to consider where she was going. In the darkness of the mezzanine she stumbled blindly against someone standing in the shadows, and involuntarily clutched at his arm to steady herself. He uttered an oath and tried to pull away from her.

The sound of his voice brought Giulia to her senses. Startled, she looked up into the face muffled by the folds of his cloak. 'Alessandro?'

She felt his arm tense beneath her fingers, and knew she was not mistaken.

'But I thought you had sailed! What are you doing here, in this house?'

'I might well ask the same question of you, Sister-in-law.' His voice was hoarse and full of menace. 'What are *you* doing here, *Giulia*?'

At the sound of her own name, she drew in her breath. 'How did you . . . ?'

'Your friend from Verona was most informative . . . after a flagon or two of wine.'

Bernardo! She might have known he would betray her, albeit unintentionally. He was too open and honest to keep a secret for long.

'If you're hoping to use this knowledge against me,' she warned, 'I must tell you that Pietro already knows the truth.'

'Ay, and has taken steps to have the marriage annulled!' Alessandro said triumphantly. 'That must distress you greatly, Sister-in-law.'

In the gloom she could see his green eyes glittering with hostility. How easily he had deceived both Francesca and herself by standing on the quayside and pretending he was about to board his brother's vessel! As for meeting him in Laura Rocco's house, she already knew he was no stranger to the courtesan. That day in St Mark's Square it had been plain they were old acquaintances. His presence here tonight could mean only one thing . . .

She said quietly, 'I warn you, Alessandro, I shall fight you every step of the way.'

He swore again beneath his breath and raised both hands to encircle her throat. She cried out in alarm and tried to break free, but he only increased the pressure until she could hear the blood thrumming in her ears. For such a slightly-built man, he seemed possessed of a surprising strength. The roaring in her ears grew louder. She felt herself gradually slipping from consciousness . . .

Then, with startling suddenness, she was released. Dimly, through a red haze of confusion, she was aware that Alessandro had been pulled roughly away from her and she heard the thud of a heavy blow, followed by the sound of running footsteps. In the next instant a strong arm went round her waist, catching her as she fell.

'Follow—him,' she gasped. 'You must see—where he goes . . .'

But her rescuer stayed where he was, lifting her high off the ground as she mercifully slid into oblivion.

She awoke to find herself in her own bed at the Ca' Gabrieli. Beside her sat a servant-girl, with face averted. As Giulia stirred, the girl turned to look at her, dark eyes concerned above the veil.

'Zoe!' Giulia's voice emerged as little more than a croak from her bruised and aching throat. 'You've come back . . .' She struggled to raise her head. 'And Kasim? It was he who rescued me! He must have been following me all day . . .'

Zoe pushed her gently but firmly back against the pillows.

'But why did you run away?' Giulia stared up at her. 'Were you afraid that Pietro would be angry when he discovered I had gone?' She saw the unhappiness in those vulnerable dark eyes and knew she had guessed right. 'I'm sorry, it was thoughtless of me.'

For answer, Zoe took her hand and pressed it against her forehead in a graceful gesture of forgiveness.

Giulia said softly, 'Once before I asked if I might see your face, and you refused. But now I know your story, Zoe. Pietro has told me what happened when you and Kasim hid him in your house. And I ask again, will you show me your face?'

The servant-girl hesitated. Then, slowly, she raised a slender hand to unfasten the veil, and let it fall.

Giulia's eyes filled with tears. The weals of red and puckered skin that marred the lower half of Zoe's face could have been caused only by severe burns. What monsters those men must have been to torture a lovely and defenceless girl, inflicting such terrible scars not only on her face but on her mind!

She replaced the veil herself, fastening it with careful fingers. 'Thank you,' she murmured. 'I pray you will not leave me again, for you and your brother are my only friends in this house.'

Zoe's eyes were eloquent above the veil. 'We—shall not—leave you,' she said in a barely audible whisper.

Giulia was much moved. She knew the effort to speak had cost Zoe dear, and could only mean that the girl now trusted her implicitly. 'I'm glad,' she said, 'for there is much to do if we're to save Pietro.' She glanced at the window and saw it was already daylight. 'I must dress . . .' But when she tried to rise, she found her head was swimming and her limbs would not obey her. 'You're right, Zoe,' she murmured, sinking wearily back against the pillows. 'First I must rest. Then I shall be better able to think what is to be done.'

Later in the day she awoke feeling much refreshed. Her brain had cleared and, apart from the darkening bruises on her throat, she seemed to have taken little harm from Alessandro's assault.

But, with her renewed strength, anger also returned. She swore vengeance against her brother-in-law, vowing he would not escape for long. Alessandro's jealousy must have been growing and festering within him for years, sparked more fiercely into life by Pietro's return from the wars. Now he realised just how lowly his own position was, destined never to marry or have power of any kind. Plainly he would stop at nothing to rid himself of his brother.

Well, he should not succeed if *she* had anything to do with it! She ordered Kasim to search the city for him—a seemingly impossible task at Carnival time—and when she had bathed, she told Zoe to bring back the dower clothes that Monna Lucia had prepared for Caterina. Among them was a gown of dark green velvet with a high collar of ruched lace that would serve to hide the bruises on her throat. She found also the fur-trimmed mantle she had worn on her arrival in Venice; at least it would make her less noticeable than Francesca's cloak of flamboyant orange.

Her first instinct was to call upon her sister-in-law and tell her all that had happened, but on second thoughts she decided against it. Francesca was fond of her younger brother: she chose to regard the faults in his character merely as a sign of youthful high spirits. Giulia could not bring herself to reveal the truth of Alessandro's treachery—at least, not until Francesca's own lively curiosity made it unavoidable. She suspected that it would not be long before her sister-in-law put in an appearance at the Ca' Gabrieli.

In the meantime she had no choice but to put her trust in Kasim. But even if he succeeded in finding Alessandro, what then? Hadn't the damage already been done? The evidence remained, spoken by Pietro to herself and overheard by at least two witnesses.

Unless *she* were to testify at the trial . . . to reveal herself as Ginette de Narbonne and strongly deny that Pietro had even mentioned his association with the Ottomans?

Procurator Martinelli listened to her plan, a dubious frown on his fleshy face. 'I fear it would avail you nothing,' he said when she had finished. 'It would be your word against theirs—and you can be sure that the witness will have been carefully chosen to give credibility to this case. Besides,' he added, 'you would be guilty of perjury.'

Giulia said unhappily, 'Then is there nothing I can do?'

He sighed. 'You had better face the truth, my dear. Your husband is guilty of treason as charged. Oh, I know that most of us in his shoes would have done the same, and probably little harm was done. But our quarrel with the Turks is of long standing and has been very bitter in the past. At present we enjoy a fragile peace, though who can say how long it will last? You cannot blame the citizens of Venice for reacting strongly to any suggestion of treason.'

'But none of this matters a fig to Alessandro!' she burst out angrily. ''Tis not a matter of politics, but a personal quarrel between brothers. He is jealous of Pietro and wants him out of the way.'

The Procurator leaned back in his chair. 'I'd like to help you, for my sister's sake,' he said with regret. 'But I don't see how it can be done.'

'You've both been very kind,' Giulia said. 'And I'm sorry to have troubled you with such an insoluble problem. Yet I still can't help feeling there *must* be a way out. Pietro himself may be able to think of something . . .' She rose to her feet. 'Please—can you arrange for me to see him again?'

The Procurator groaned. 'It was far from easy the first time!'

'But you're a very eminent man, my lord. I know you can do it if you try.'

'And you're a very strong-willed young woman! However, I must confess that doesn't altogether surprise me. Come, let us see what we can do.'

The gaoler met them at the door, his face far from encouraging. The prisoner was being difficult, he told them. He would not eat or move from his bed, nor would he speak a word to anyone.

'He will surely wish to speak to his wife,' the Procurator said. 'Fetch him to us at once, if you please.'

The gaoler shrugged and went away. Two minutes later he returned alone. 'No use,' he said, with some satisfaction. 'He refuses to stir from his cell.'

'Then I will visit him there,' said Giulia, and before the gaoler could stop her she had slipped past him down the dark and gloomy passage.

The man had left the cell door open, since the occupant showed no desire to leave. It was a small, cramped chamber with damp walls and a straw-covered floor. What little light there was came from a high barred window. Amidst the gloom Giulia could just make out the huddled figure lying upon the bunk.

'Pietro?' she said uncertainly. When there was no reply, she advanced further into the cell. 'I must talk to you. It's important . . .'

He groaned, flinging his arm across his face. 'Go away, damn you, and leave me in peace.'

Giulia flinched. This was even worse than she had feared. 'I know who your enemy is,' she said, gazing helplessly down at his inert form. 'That's what I've come to tell you.'

'I have many enemies,' he said, his voice muffled.

'But only one who's responsible for your present plight!' She fought to control her impatience. ''Tis your own brother—Alessandro. He did not sail with your ship as we thought . . . that was merely a trick to persuade us he had left the city. Last night I saw him at—at a house in the town and, when I challenged him, he tried to kill me. Look, if you don't believe me . . .' She bent closer, pulling the collar away from her neck.

With a sigh he uncovered his eyes to study the bruises dark against her ivory skin. 'I believe you,' he said dispassionately.

'It was Kasim who came to my rescue, and now he has gone in search of Alessandro. When we find him . . .'

'My dear, you're wasting your time. It cannot possibly have been Alessandro who denounced me to the Council. I told you, I spent that night . . .'

'At the house of Laura Rocco!' she interrupted fiercely. 'The very same place where I encountered Alessandro last night, on the stairs. Surely that *proves* there's some connection between them?'

Now at last she had his full attention. He raised himself on his elbows to stare at her. '*You* went to the house of Laura Rocco?'

'My lord, I'm not a complete fool!' She sat on the edge of his bunk, speaking with urgency. 'I overheard you make an assignation with her outside the entrance to the convent. That's how I guessed where you had spent that night.'

He frowned, obviously perplexed. Now that her eyes were growing accustomed to the gloom, Giulia could see the two days' growth of beard upon his chin, the dark shadows beneath his eyes. She longed to touch him, to take him in her arms and restore his will to live; yet she dared not while the barrier between them remained—the barrier that was Ginette de Narbonne.

She continued, 'When you were with—with the Frenchwoman, there must have been some kind of listening device in the wall. Everything you said to her was overheard by whoever was in the next room.'

'*Laura Rocco* told you this?'

'Not in so many words. But when I accused her, she made no attempt to deny it.' She gazed at him pleadingly. 'Don't you *see*? Alessandro had planned the whole thing—and no doubt paid Laura Rocco well for her complicity.'

'Ay, and they were clever enough to find the one woman capable of undermining my defences?' Pietro's voice was bleak with bitterness. 'How cleverly she played her part, disarming me with her love-making and encouraging me to talk . . .'

Giulia turned cold. She stared down at her gloved hands, saying nothing.

'You should not have gone there,' he said curtly. 'I fear by doing so you may have placed yourself in considerable danger.'

''Tis not *my* danger that concerns me!' she retorted, grateful for the change of subject. 'But how we are to construct your defence.'

'You know very well I *have* no defence.'

'Oh, how can you accept defeat so easily?' Tears of frustration started to her eyes. 'Now that we know who your enemy is, we must fight back!'

He shook his head wonderingly. 'I don't understand you, Giulia. Heaven knows you have little to thank me for, yet you seem intent upon saving me, I cannot imagine why.'

'Because I love you,' she said simply, knowing she had nothing to lose.

He stared searchingly into her eyes, then sighed. 'I believe you do. The pity of it is that it comes too late. I've nothing to offer you now, surely you realise that?'

'Oh, my lord . . .!' Unable to stop herself, she caught his hand and pressed it to her breast. 'I *can* obtain your release, I'm certain of it! And when you're free, then I shall prove how much I love you. Only trust me . . .'

'Giulia . . .' Gently but firmly he detached his hand from her grasp and raised it to touch her cheek. 'You're so lovely . . . but every time I look at you I see only her. Once she reminded me of you, and that's why I took her, to satisfy the hunger I felt for you. Now I fear it would be the other way round—and I would not wish to use you for such a purpose.' He sank back wearily. 'That's why you'd much better give up this hopeless attempt to rescue me and go home to your father.'

'I cannot do that.' She rose to her feet. 'Indeed, I'm resolved to rescue you—whether you wish to be rescued or not!'

For the first time since she had walked into his cell, he managed the glimmer of a smile. 'Oh, my dear . . . how I wish I had recognised my good fortune when I married you! What a fool I've been . . .'

She bit back the retort that sprang to her lips, and turned to the door.

'Giulia . . .' There was a note of genuine concern in his voice. 'Take care.'

So he was not completely uninterested in what became of her! The knowledge gave her new heart. She did not look back, but left the cell with head held high, ignoring the long-faced gaoler lurking just outside the door.

Procurator Martinelli turned to her curiously. 'You look pleased, madonna. Have you learned something that may be of some use?'

She shook her head. 'Tell me, my lord—if I could persuade my brother-in-law to retract his accusation, would the case against Pietro be dropped?'

'It's possible, I suppose . . . provided the witnesses could also be made to withdraw. But how do you propose to achieve this miracle?'

'I'm not sure.' She set her chin at a resolute angle. 'First I have to find Alessandro. Then I'll set about making him change his mind.'

Giulia returned to the Ca' Gabrieli riding high on a wave of determination, but, as time went on, that determination began to waver. Day after day Kasim returned, answering her question with a shake of the head. It seemed Alessandro had completely disappeared into the bewildering maze that was Venice.

One thing that puzzled her greatly was the continuing absence of Francesca. She could not understand why her sister-in-law should be avoiding her. Unless . . .

Supposing Francesca was protecting Alessandro—even hiding him in her house? It seemed unlikely that she would knowingly conspire with him against Pietro, but he could easily have spun her some fabrication to explain why he wished to stay secretly in Venice. And now that he knew the truth of Giulia's identity, he might well use it to turn his sister against her. Convinced that she was right, Giulia sent Kasim to keep watch day and night on Francesca's house.

In the meantime she asked her husband's steward to take her on a conducted tour of the Ca' Gabrieli. There were far more rooms than she had realised, many of them sadly in need of redecoration. The steward seemed pleased by her interest. Indeed, it surprised her how willingly the servants accepted her as their mistress. Perhaps having so recently been a servant herself gave her a certain advantage, since she was aware how they would judge her. She must not be harsh and unbending like Monna Lucia, she decided; but neither must she be too easy-going, for then they would not respect her. Finding the middle way was a challenge that helped to pass away the long hours of inactivity.

Worse than the boredom, however, was the loneliness. The house seemed so large, and her own position so isolated. She wandered aimlessly through the empty rooms, longing to hear the sound of voices. In the library she thought of Gentile and how they had played hide-and-seek together. If only he was still here . . .

At the recollection of that final scene with Cardinal Benetti and his sister, anger came flooding back. They had no right to take the child away from his home! If poor Gentile had been unhappy before, in the sole care of Monna Clarissa, how much worse must it be for him now, in that austere household dominated by his autocratic uncle. Giulia made up her mind to go the Benettis at once and demand to see her stepson. Surely they could not refuse?

The Cardinal received her in a sombre chamber hung with paintings of impressive size and magnificence. Scenes of martyrdom abounded, she noticed. He gestured her to a high-backed chair facing the flaring light of a candelabrum, while taking care to seat himself in the shadows.

'This is a most unexpected pleasure,' he remarked in his quiet, beautifully modulated voice. 'May I ask what brings you here, madonna?'

'I was anxious about Gentile,' she replied. 'I came to find out if he is well and happy.'

'You can be assured that now we have him safe in my house his upbringing will give no further cause for concern.'

'I'm glad to hear it, my lord. But I should still like to see him, if you've no objection?'

'I fear that will not be possible.' The Cardinal's tone was final.

'May I ask why?'

'It would be unsettling for the child. 'Tis best he should be allowed to forget his unfortunate connection with the Gabrielis.'

'But Gentile *is* a Gabrieli,' Giulia pointed out, keeping her voice even. 'And when his father returns home . . .'

'Ha!' The Cardinal uttered a short laugh. 'But his father, I think, will *not* be returning home! This time Pietro Gabrieli will be made to answer for his sins, since he is at last revealed for what he is—a traitor who had made a pact with the Devil.'

Giulia flushed angrily. 'That's nonsense. The Sultan was kind to him . . .'

'The Devil is often kind, but in return he demands a man's heart and soul.' He leant towards her, and as the candlelight illumined his face she saw the leaping flame reflected in his eyes—the burning eyes of a fanatic. 'Pietro Gabrieli is damned! I knew it as soon as he came back to Venice. That's why I was determined to remove Gentile from his father's clutches.'

She stared at him helplessly. 'Have you no compassion? Let me see the child, I beg you. I'm very fond of Gentile—surely you can't imagine I would do him any harm?'

'Those who associate with evil must of necessity themselves become contaminated.' He sat back in the shadows again, only the drumming of his long fingers on the curved arm of his chair betraying his emotion. 'You had better go, madonna.'

She stood up, hiding her clenched fists within the folds of her cloak. 'Very well. But I warn you, I don't intend to give up until Gentile is restored to his rightful home.'

He made no reply, but moved swiftly across the room to fling open the door. 'This lady is leaving,' he told the servant waiting outside. 'Show her out—and on no account is she to be admitted to my house again.'

Seething with resentment, Giulia walked past him, not daring to look again into that grim, skull-like countenance for fear of losing her temper.

To add insult to injury, the servant showed her out of a side entrance on to a narrow street some way from where her gondola was waiting. Before she could protest, however, the door was slammed shut behind her. Furious, she turned away and began walking towards the Piazza, so preoccupied with her thoughts that she almost failed to recognise the woman who brushed past her in the gathering dusk. It was perhaps the coincidence that brought her up with a jerk—for she suddenly realised this was the very spot, a few yards from the landward gate of the convent, where Pietro had made his assignation with Laura Rocco.

Laura Rocco . . . !

Giulia wheeled round to stare after the tall, graceful figure hurrying away from her. For once, the courtesan was masked and heavily cloaked, plainly not wishing to attract attention. She made her way along the narrow street to the house Giulia had just left, then stopped to glance furtively over her shoulder before knocking on the door. Giulia pressed back against the wall, watching in fascination.

Laura Rocco . . . calling upon Cardinal Benetti?

What on earth could the most notorious courtesan in Venice have to say to that most pious of churchmen? Giulia could think of only one topic they might possibly have in common . . .

Without giving herself time to consider, she stepped out from her hiding-place, intending to challenge Laura before she could enter the Cardinal's house, but in the next instant she was seized from behind and pulled back against the wall. For a moment she was too startled even to struggle, but as she opened her mouth to scream, her captor clapped a hand over her face.

'*Keep quiet!*'

The voice in her ear was Alessandro's.

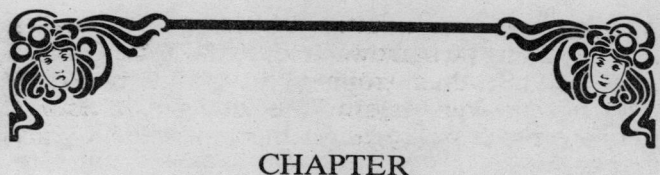

CHAPTER TWELVE

'KEEP QUIET—or you'll ruin everything!' Alessandro's grip tightened. 'Let her go into the house. Then we can catch them together.'

It took Giulia a moment to grasp the full meaning of his words. She stopped struggling at once.

'Giulia?' Cautiously he took his hand away from her mouth. 'Do you understand what I'm saying?'

'I understand.' She turned her head to look at him. His light green eyes were brilliant with excitement but no longer held the hostility she had seen there before. Behind him in the shadows stood another figure, tall and bearded. 'Kasim!' she gasped.

'I found him watching my sister's house,' Alessandro said. 'I gather you'd sent him to discover where I was hiding.'

She said slowly, 'I thought it was you who'd betrayed Pietro . . .'

'And *I* thought it was *you*!' His tone was grim. 'But now we both know differently, don't we?'

Giulia glanced along the narrow street. There was no sign of Laura Rocco. 'Look! She must have gone inside . . .'

'In that case it's time for us to join them.' He took Giulia's arm, signalling Kasim to follow.

Outside the door, she warned, 'The Cardinal's given orders I'm not to be admitted.'

'Has he indeed?' Alessandro smiled, resting his hand on the hilt of his sword. 'Well, we shan't let that stop us!' He gave the bell-rope a determined pull, beckoning Kasim to stand on the other side of the doorway.

The door was opened by the same servant who had so humiliatingly seen her off the premises a few minutes ago.

'My name is Gabrieli,' Alessandro announced, 'and I've urgent business with the Cardinal.'

The servant regarded him doubtfully. Then his eye fell on Giulia and grew dark, but before he had time to protest, Kasim crooked a massive arm around his neck and dragged him into the shadows. There came the sound of a blow, followed by a muffled thud. Kasim stepped forward, his face as inscrutable as ever.

'Quick!' Alessandro pushed Giulia before him into the entrance. 'Can you remember the way?'

'I think so . . .'

She led them up the stairs to the portego. Here a footman stepped forward to challenge them, but on seeing the huge Turk with his curved dagger he shrank back against the wall, his face blanched with fear.

'Which room?' demanded Alessandro.

Giulia pointed to the door.

He stood with his ear against it, then gave her a swift nod. 'They're arguing. We shall catch them unawares.'

She felt a surge of exhilaration. 'Let me go first!'

After a moment's hesitation, he said, 'Very well . . . but I shall be close on your heels. Kasim can keep guard outside.'

She flung open the door. The two people inside the room swung round to stare at her.

For a second or two there was a stunned silence, then Laura Rocco turned on the Cardinal. 'What did I tell you? *She*'s the one . . .'

'The lady is known to me,' he interrupted smoothly. His gaze slid to Alessandro, who had closed the door behind them. 'And so is her brother-in-law.'

'Her *brother-in-law?*' Astonishment showed on the courtesan's beautiful face.

'Yes, I am wife to Pietro Gabrieli,' Giulia said proudly. 'And an unwitting tool in your plot to destroy him.'

Laura's eyes narrowed. 'You played your part willingly enough.'

Giulia, flushing, ignored the jibe. 'When I asked you who was the listener in the next room, you refused to tell me.' She looked at the Cardinal. 'But now I think my question is answered.'

He returned her gaze, his calm unruffled. 'Do you accuse me of conspiring against your husband, madonna? If so, I fear you're mistaken. My business with this lady is of an entirely spiritual nature. Even a harlot may seek absolution for her sins.'

Alessandro gave a short bark of disbelieving laughter. Giulia laid a restraining hand on his arm, and addressed the Cardinal. 'Monna Laura's conscience must be troubling her indeed if she cannot wait to see you in the confessional but must come hurrying here to your house at this late hour. Does she repent, I wonder, of the damage she has done?'

Laura Rocco drew her cloak closer about her. 'What passes between my confessor and myself is a private matter. Now, if you'll excuse me . . .' She moved towards the door.

'Not yet, madonna.' Alessandro barred her way.

'Why, you've only this minute arrived! And we have much to discuss.'

Her attempt to escape frustrated, the courtesan turned impatiently to Cardinal Benetti. 'For pity's sake put an end to this farce! Summon your servants to throw them out.'

'Summon them by all means,' Alessandro retorted. 'Though I think you'll find them powerless to obey. We did not come alone.'

The Cardinal regarded him impassively, but Giulia saw a nerve twitch in his jaw and knew that he was by no means as confident as he appeared. Encouraged, she said, 'My lord, I fear your reputation is at stake. Until now you've been regarded as a man of virtue whose morals are beyond reproach. Indeed, 'tis on those very grounds you saw fit to take Gentile from his father's house—and tonight refused to let me see him. Those who associate with evil, you said, themselves become contaminated. How would you like it known, I wonder, that you were discovered here this evening closeted privately with the most notorious courtesan in all Venice?'

The Cardinal was visibly disturbed. He hissed to Laura Rocco, 'You should not have come! I told you . . .'

'*And*, moreover,' Giulia continued mercilessly, 'that you recently spent an entire night in her house, in one of the upstairs rooms! Where would your precious reputation be then?'

He stared at her with undisguised hatred. 'No one would listen to you.'

'They will when I give evidence at my husband's trial. Then the whole Council will hear what happened on that night. It may not save Pietro, but it will assuredly reveal *you* as a hypocrite of the worst possible kind, my lord Cardinal!'

'Do you honestly think they would believe your word against mine?' he demanded furiously.

'Perhaps not. But I still doubt you'd care to have it made public knowledge. There's no smoke without fire, they say. People will listen—and remember. They'll never again hear your name without saying, 'Cardinal Benetti . . . was he not involved in some scandal?' She let her words sink in before adding quietly, 'Of course, if you were to retract your accusation . . . ?'

'Bravo!' Alessandro muttered in her ear.

The Cardinal shot her a haunted look, gnawing his lip.

'Don't listen to her,' Laura urged. 'She can't possibly prove that you were in my house that night. No one saw you . . .'

'Be quiet!' He turned to Giulia again, speaking in a low, carefully controlled tone. 'If I retract my accusation, what then?'

'My husband will be released from prison.' Watching his face, Giulia could see the battle taking place in his mind. She went on, 'And you'll allow Gentile to return home immediately. I believe your concern for him is genuine, my lord, but I give you my word he'll be safe in my care.'

The Cardinal was silent.

'This has nought to do with me,' Laura muttered, once again attempting to push past Alessandro. 'I'm leaving . . .'

'Let her go,' Giulia commanded.

He stepped back obediently, opening the door with a show of mock-gallantry. 'We shall be sorry to lose you, madonna—but no doubt you've a busy night's work ahead!'

The oath she uttered beneath her breath could

be heard only by Alessandro. He grinned appreciatively and closed the door behind her.

'Come, my lord Cardinal,' he said. 'You've heard what my sister-in-law proposes. Give us your word that you'll withdraw your accusation and we'll leave you in peace.'

The Cardinal sank into his chair, burying his head in his hands. 'You have my word,' he muttered, his voice harsh with despair. 'Take the child—and go!'

In the gondola, Giulia sat with her arm around Gentile, holding him close. He was still a little bemused by what had happened, but his joy when Giulia told him she was taking him home had been almost pitiful to behold. For only the second time in his life he had dared to disobey Monna Clarissa, tearing himself away from her grasp when she sought to detain him. His small face had been scarlet with defiance: even now he still trembled within the circle of Giulia's arm. She looked across his head to Alessandro. 'You don't think the Cardinal will go back on his word?'

He shook his head. 'He will not dare, for fear of what you might say if Pietro is brought to trial. You have him in a cleft stick.' His eyes were warm with admiration. 'You were magnificent, Sister-in-law!'

She smiled at him. 'Oh, Alessandro—can you ever forgive me? I was so sure it was you who had conspired with Laura Rocco, especially when I saw you at her house that night.'

'I'd followed you there,' he said. 'From the moment Bernardo revealed you were not who you pretended to be I became suspicious. And when you threatened to fight me every step of the way then I fear I lost my temper. For that I must beg your forgiveness, but I was convinced you were involved in the plot against my brother.'

'And that's what you told Francesca?'

He nodded. 'She was horrified. She thought you'd tricked her into helping you.'

'No wonder she hasn't come to visit me,' Giulia said. 'I guessed she must be hiding you. That's why I sent Kasim to watch her house.'

'It's as well you did. When I realised he was helping you, I began to doubt my own judgment. Kasim's loyalty to Pietro is beyond question. And he's no fool, even though he may lack a tongue to express himself.' Alessandro grinned. 'It took me a while to persuade him that I meant no harm to my brother. Despite the differences between us, I've no intention of following in my uncle's footsteps!'

'I thought you were jealous of Pietro,' Giulia confessed.

'I am,' he said frankly. ''Tis not easy to be a younger brother in Venice. But I've spent too long trying to stifle my resentment by whoring and drinking myself senseless. Now I've decided to make a life of my own . . . in another town, if necessary. I shall go to Milan—or perhaps even Rome—to try my fortune.'

'I think you're very wise,' Giulia said. 'As long as you stay here, you'll always be living in Pietro's shadow.'

'Ay, and watching him daily grow more enamoured of his wife,' Alessandro said wryly. 'To see you constantly together—and enjoying the kind of life I can never have—would be more than I can bear.'

Giulia's face clouded. 'You see my future more clearly than I do. I fear Pietro may send me away . . .'

'How can you say such a thing? When he finds himself free—and learns 'tis all thanks to you—he will surely count himself the luckiest man alive?'

'It isn't quite so simple as that,' she said with a sigh. 'You see, he fancies himself in love with someone else.'

'What if he does? All Venetians fall in and out of love frequently, especially at Carnival time. 'Tis part of the fun. But you're his *wife*, Giulia—and that's a different matter entirely.'

She fell silent, toying with the ring on her finger. It was true she was now Pietro's wife, in fact as well as in name, but would he ever forgive her for practising such a deception upon him? Filled with doubt, she hugged Gentile even closer.

On the following day Procurator Martinelli came to tell her that the case against Pietro had been dropped. 'I don't know how you achieved this remarkable feat,' he said, 'and perhaps I had better not ask. But I understand a certain dignitary of the church has intervened on your husband's behalf.'

Giulia lowered her eyes discreetly. 'This is welcome news, my lord. May I ask when Pietro will be released?'

'Within a day or so, I imagine.' He raised her hand to his lips. 'I wish you well, madonna, and hope we meet again under happier circumstances.'

She smiled at him warmly, a little surprised by the friendliness of his manner. 'I hope so too, my lord.'

It was Alessandro who went to meet his brother from gaol and bring him home. 'Be careful what you say,' Giulia pleaded before he left. 'You may tell him about the Cardinal if you wish, but I'd prefer you left the rest to me.'

'I understand,' said Alessandro, smiling. 'And I

promise not to spoil your moment of glory.' He bent to kiss her on the cheek before going down to the gondola.

Glory? It would hardly be that, Giulia thought with a sinking heart. She had rehearsed her confession over and over again, but still could not imagine how Pietro was likely to react. Admittedly he had declared himself in love with Ginette de Narbonne, but would he be so glad to find himself married to her? No matter how romantic his feelings he might still regard her as being a far from suitable wife and mother for his children. And would he not resent strongly being trapped in a situation he could not escape?

She prepared herself to receive him in the portego, the servants arrayed behind her, Gentile at her side. Her gown was of cream embroidered satin and Zoe had dressed her hair in a crown of tiny plaits, threaded with pearls. As a precaution, she removed the ring of approval from her finger and hid it within the bodice of her gown. She had no wish for him to see it before she was ready.

At the sound of footsteps on the stair she rose to her feet, trying to still her beating heart. A small hand crept into hers and, glancing down into Gentile's anxious face, she realised she was not alone in her nervousness. She gave him a smile of encouragement and squeezed his hand.

Pietro's head was bowed as he mounted the topmost stair, followed by his brother and Kasim. He looked thin and haggard, his shoulders stooped with weariness.

Giulia stepped forward, holding Gentile tightly by the hand. 'We're glad to see you home, my lord,' she murmured, dropping a low curtsy. 'Gentile, bid your father welcome.'

But Gentile, staring up at the tall figure of his father, was too overcome to say a word. His lower lip trembled ominously. It was Pietro who saved the situation by kneeling to kiss his son on both cheeks. Giulia, watching him, saw that for once he could not hide his emotion. Tears glittered in his eyes as he straightened.

'You need rest, my lord,' she said quickly. 'I've had your room made ready, if you wish to retire at once.'

He turned to look at her, his expression unfathomable. 'Alessandro tells me that my release is entirely due to your efforts. Please accept my gratitude for what you've done.'

His tone was coldly, formally, polite. Giulia lowered her lashes to hide her mortification. 'I warned you, my lord, that I meant to rescue you, come what may.'

'So you did,' he conceded. 'Though I confess I'm at a loss to understand exactly how you achieved my release.'

''Tis a long story,' she said with an attempt at lightness. 'I shall tell you later, when you're rested.'

'Very well.' He turned away. Behind his back, Giulia exchanged an uneasy glance with Alessandro, who shrugged his shoulders.

Still holding Gentile's hand, she called a footman to take Pietro's cloak, and bade Kasim escort him to his room. If Pietro was surprised to see her so evidently in charge of his household he gave no sign of it, but took his leave of her with as courteous a bow as any wife could wish.

When he had gone, she turned to Alessandro. 'He still seems rather strange,' she said. 'Did he say anything to you on the journey?'

'He hardly spoke. I told him of our visit to the Cardinal, but he hardly bothered to listen. It was as if the matter did not even interest him.'

'I expect that's because he's tired,' she said, frowning. 'When he's slept and eaten he'll feel differently.'

Pray heaven that he may! she added privately, thinking she would rather bear his anger than have him continue to treat her with such unflattering apathy.

On returning to her own room she bathed and let Zoe anoint her with perfumed oils until her skin took on a silken sheen. Then she called for one of the eastern gowns Pietro had once ordered her to wear, and loosened her hair so that it hung in golden waves about her shoulders. Finally she slipped his ring back on her finger before taking up a consciously seductive pose on the divan, well aware that the diaphanous gown of silver gauze clung to every line and curve of her body. Now, she thought, I'm ready to banish Ginette de Narbonne once and for all from his memory!

But as the minutes ticked by, and then the hours, and still he did not come, the pose was forgotten. Gradually she slipped back against the cushions, her head drooping, until at last she fell into a light, uneasy sleep.

She awoke with a start to find she was no longer alone. Pietro stood at the foot of the divan, looking down at her.

'My lord!' She struggled to sit up. 'I didn't hear you come in . . .'

His eyes were enigmatic as they rested on her flushed face before travelling down to where the tips of her pointed breasts showed clearly through the transparent gauze. 'It surprises me to find you dressed in such a manner,' he said abruptly. 'I thought that during my absence you'd returned to more conventional fashions.'

'I—I wanted to please you, my lord,' she said, still too startled by his sudden appearance to think coherently.

'You've always pleased me, Giulia.' His voice was cold, belying his words. 'As well you know.'

Her heart leapt. She slid from the divan to stand before him, but with a groan he swung away from her, putting some distance between them. When he turned his face was pale and set. ''Twould be all too easy for me to take you now, like some worthless whore—but if I did, I'd never forgive myself. I owe you my life, Giulia. That's something I cannot forget. And the only way I can possibly repay you is by giving you your freedom.'

'No!' Trembling, she forced herself to speak more calmly. 'If you're still thinking in terms of an annulment, then I must tell you that it's impossible, for we are truly husband and wife.'

He stared at her. 'What nonsense is this?'

'It's not nonsense, I assure you—and I have this to prove it.' She held out her hand.

He dragged his eyes away from her face to look closely at the ring on her finger. ''Tis indeed mine,' he murmured, frowning. 'But how did it come to be in your possession?'

'You gave it to me, my lord. Do you not remember?'

He stiffened. 'I fear you're mistaken. I gave it to someone else entirely.'

She raised her sleeve to cover half her face and looked up at him, speaking with the voice of Ginette de Narbonne. 'Do you not recognise me, monsieur? Perhaps it was my accent that deceived you . . .'

He started back, his face ashen.

Giulia dropped her sleeve, and spoke in her normal voice. 'I played a trick on you, my lord, and for that I'm sorry. But I was desperate to save our marriage. That was my only reason for going to Laura Rocco's house, I beg you to believe me.'

'*You*?' He was looking at her as if she were a total stranger. 'You were the Frenchwoman . . . ?'

She nodded, her throat too dry to speak.

'I should have guessed,' he said slowly. 'I should have known it couldn't be any other woman. The shape of your mouth, the turn of your head . . . everything gave you away.'

'If you'd asked me to take off my mask I should have been discovered at once,' she said. 'But you insisted I left it on . . .'

'Because I wanted to pretend she was you!' He stepped closer, searching her face. 'I couldn't believe my good fortune in finding someone so like the woman who obsessed me; but I was afraid that if I saw her face the illusion would be destroyed.'

There was a light in his eyes that made her suddenly breathless. 'No doubt you're wondering why I encouraged you to talk,' she went on quickly. 'That was Laura Rocco's idea. She said it pleased men to talk after they had made love and I—I believed her. That's why I let you tell me about the Sultan. It didn't occur to me that there might be someone listening in the next room, I swear it! I never dreamed . . .'

Without warning, he raised a hand to encircle her neck, the pressure of his thumb forcing her face upwards until it was only an inch or two from his own. She sensed the barely controlled passion in his grip, but could not tell whether it was prompted by anger or desire.

In her nervousness she babbled on, 'I—I would have told you before, but I knew you thought the Frenchwoman responsible for your arrest. The only way I could prove my innocence was by obtaining your release.' She tried to read his expression, but found it impossible. 'You do believe me, my lord?'

'I believe you.' He spoke mechanically, as if only half attending.

'And you're not too angry with me?'

'What man would not be angry to discover his wife had played such a trick on him?' His voice was menacingly quiet. 'Did you expect me to forgive you meekly . . . and take no further action?'

Giulia gazed up at him in fascination, her lips parted. 'What—what do you mean to do?'

'I fear I shall have to punish you, my dear.' He pulled her roughly against him, the touch of his hands searing through the thin stuff of her gown. 'And 'tis no use pleading for a delay . . .'

She gave a cry of alarm as he swept her off the ground. He carried her swiftly across the room and almost threw her on to the bed, tearing off her flimsy robe in a single motion to lay bare her smooth and glistening body. Then, with a groan, he was upon her.

Giulia smiled, relaxed and sensuous as a cat. 'If this is punishment, my lord,' she murmured against the warm flesh of Pietro's shoulder, 'then I warn you that I shall try to make you angry with me more often.'

'Minx!' He eased himself away from her to lie on his back, his eyes closed. 'When I think of that night in Laura Rocco's house . . . You realise the Frenchwoman had me quite bewitched?'

'I know.' She propped herself up on one elbow so that she could gaze lovingly down into his lean, hawklike face. 'To be honest, I was more than a little jealous of her.'

'And what of that ageing, neglectful husband she complained about? I suppose that was me!'

'I never said he was ageing. It was you who jumped to that conclusion.'

'Only because I could not conceive how any normal, hot-blooded man could leave untouched so desirable a wife.' He opened his eyes to stare up into her face, still flushed and tremulous from his love-making. 'I must have been mad!'

'Then . . . you forgive me?'

'I forgive Ginette. I haven't yet made up my mind about Giulia.' He gave her a quizzical look. 'Whatever put such an outrageous scheme into your head?'

She sat up. 'Wait—I shall show you.' Naked, she slipped from the bed and ran across the room to fetch the *Decameron Nights*.

When she returned, he raised his head inquiringly. 'What have you there?'

'The book you allowed me to borrow from your library. I'm going to read you a story.'

'Must you?' He reached out a hand to fondle her breast. 'I'm hardly in the mood to listen to stories.'

'This one is different. I'll believe you'll find it of particular interest.' She found the place with ease, since it was already marked, and began to read, skipping some of the longer passages.

He listened soberly, his face giving nothing away. When she had finished, he remarked, 'I've always suspected it was dangerous for women to read stories. Now I'm certain of it!'

She closed the book and laid it aside. 'It's only because men are so obstinate that women must resort to such subterfuges. Like me, Ginette had to trick her husband into giving her the ring—or be cast aside.'

'In the story, Ginette not only acquired her husband's ring,' he observed. 'She also succeeded in bearing him a son.'

Giulia flushed. ''Tis too soon to be certain, my lord. But if I did . . .' She looked at him anxiously. 'You wouldn't mind too much?'

'I'd be overjoyed.' His eyes narrowed. 'What makes you think otherwise?'

'The circumstances of my birth haven't changed. I still don't know who was my mother.' She lowered her eyes, unable to confess she had once thought it was Laura Rocco. 'There are thousands of courtesans in Venice. She could be any one of them—provided, of course, she's still alive.'

For a long moment he regarded her silently as she sat amid the tumbled bedclothes, her skin warm in the candlelight against the white of the sheets, her hair a nimbus of gold framing the small, piquant face. When at last he spoke, his tone was gentle. 'One thing is certain, my love. You did not inherit your strength of character from your father. Whoever your mother was, she must have been a remarkable woman.'

Giulia said sadly, 'If only I knew . . .'

'Put it out of your mind.' He drew her towards him, cradling her against his bare chest. 'These things need not concern you now. You're my wife and that's enough.'

She pulled back a little so that she could look into his face. 'My lord . . .'

'Pietro,' he corrected, absently caressing her spine with his free hand.

'Pietro, I've told you twice that I love you . . .'

'So you have.' His exploring fingers found the curve of her hip. 'And I confess myself gratified.'

'But you've never . . .' She broke off with an involuntary gasp of pleasure as his touch became more purposeful, but obstinately refused to be diverted. 'My lord, you're being deliberately annoying! You know very well what it is I want to hear.'

'And *you* know very well the answer!' His smiling mouth hovered above her own. 'Indeed, love is an inadequate word for what I feel for you at this moment, Giulia . . .'

'Yet it would please me greatly to hear you say it.'

He said it, and then proceeded to demonstrate the truth of his avowal in as convincing and enjoyable a manner as she could wish.

Early on Ascension Day, while the citizens of Venice were getting ready for the most important feast-day of the year, Caterina Tebaldi was married at last to her Bernardo. The ceremony took place quietly in the chapel of S. Cecilia's Convent, a small oasis of calm away from the excited crowds swarming through the streets outside. The bride, wearing a loose-fitting gown that cleverly concealed her advanced state of pregnancy, had never looked so well or so happy. Her father too was in excellent spirits, though this may have been partly due to the recent delivery of a consignment of gold and silver thread from the Orient. Even her mother seemed resigned to the situation.

Giulia was amazed to see that Monna Lucia had

decided to attend. Her first sight of that sour, thin-lipped countenance aroused all her old feelings of fear and resentment, but Pietro's warm hand gripping her elbow restored her confidence.

After the ceremony, when they were gathered in the convent parlour for refreshment, Giulia found herself face-to-face with her former mistress, and said impulsively, 'I'm glad you came, madonna—for Caterina's sake.'

'It was my duty to be present.' Monna Lucia's icy gaze swept over Giulia's costly gown embroidered with loops of seed-pearls. 'It seems *you*'ve done well for yourself, madam. I trust you appreciate how fortunate you are.' Her eyes flickered to Pietro, who was engaged in conversation with Ercole. 'Particularly since Messer Gabrieli seems prepared to overlook your lack of breeding.'

Giulia drew in her breath, but before she could even attempt to reply, the Prioress had stepped forward to confront Monna Lucia. 'Whatever good fortune Giulia may have,' she said firmly, 'she has entirely deserved. Her husband, I know, has come to value her highly for those qualities of love and unshakeable loyalty she has brought to their marriage.'

'Quite so, Mother.' Monna Lucia, plainly overawed by the nun's commanding presence, dropped an obsequious curtsy. 'And may I take this opportunity to thank you personally for all the care and attention you have given my daughter Caterina?'

The Prioress bowed graciously in acceptance. Above Monna Lucia's head she exchanged a conspiratorial look with Giulia, but before they had a chance to speak, Caterina approached. Ignoring her mother, she begged Giulia to come and help her to change out of her bridal gown.

'We leave for Padua tomorrow,' she told her excitedly when they were alone. 'The Prioress has helped Bernardo to find a post at the university.'

'That's wonderful news!' Giulia noticed the pronounced curve of Caterina's belly beneath her thin shift, and smiled. 'Before you go, there's something I want to tell you. I too am expecting a child . . .'

'Oh, Giulia!' Caterina flung her arms around her half-sister. 'I'm so glad for you . . .' She drew back, looking seriously into her face. 'I shall never be able to thank you enough for sending Bernardo to find me. Why, if it were not for you . . .'

'Be as happy as I am, that's all I ask.'

'*Are* you happy, Giulia?' Caterina sounded doubtful. 'Pietro Gabrieli seems so proud, so unapproachable. I'm glad *I* didn't have to marry him, for he would frighten me half to death!'

'Then we are both content,' said Giulia, laughing. 'For *I* can't imagine being married to anyone else!'

And indeed that was true, she thought, glancing sideways at her husband as they left the convent to mingle with the crowds in St Mark's Square. They had grown so close in the last few weeks, so completely united in mind and body, that it seemed almost as if they could read each other's thoughts. At this very moment, for example, she sensed that he had something on his mind and was uncertain whether to tell her.

'What is it?' she asked, leaning close so that he could hear her above the noise. 'Have you had orders to sail?'

'Not yet, though it cannot be long.' He put his arm round her, protecting her from the jostling throng. 'Come, let's try to find Francesca and

Alessandro. They said they would bring Gentile down to the Riva degli Schiavoni so that he would have a good view of the State galley.'

She said nothing more, putting the matter aside while they joined the rest of his family. Together they watched the Doge sail out into the lagoon to cast his ring into the water, symbolising the annual marriage of Venice to the Adriatic. But later, when they were returning home by gondola, she tried again. 'I know you've something to tell me, my love. Why do you hesitate?'

'Because I'm not sure it's wise, after all this time.' He looked up to see her eyes fixed beseechingly on him, and sighed. 'Today, while you were with Caterina, the Prioress took me aside and told me something she thought I ought to know. It had troubled her greatly, she said, to hear you reviled by Monna Lucia for lack of breeding. She had not intended to speak out, but felt that now she must.'

Giulia stared at him, hardly daring to breathe. 'Was it . . . about my mother?'

He nodded. 'Apparently she was very young, and of a noble family. Your father must have been a handsome man in his youth and she fell in love with him, though it wasn't long before she realised that marriage between them would be a disaster. She sent him away—and only then discovered she was pregnant. Like Caterina, she was forced by her family to enter a convent, and when her child was born it was taken away from her to be raised in the foundling hospital. Later she came to regret this bitterly, and sent word to your father, begging him to come for the child and bring her up in his own home.'

Giulia said slowly, 'I've often wondered why he

did that. It seemed so much out of character. But what happened to *her* . . . my mother?'

'She chose to stay where she was, in the convent.'

'She became a nun?' Sudden anger overwhelmed her. 'And my father told me she was a "woman of Venice"! How dared he say such a thing to deceive me . . . ?'

'My sweet love, he dared not tell you anything else?' Pietro took her in his arms and held her close. 'But he never ceased to admire and respect your mother—and when he discovered Caterina was pregnant, it was to her that he inevitably turned for help.'

Giulia pulled away from him. 'You cannot mean . . . ?'

Tenderly Pietro pushed a strand of hair back from her forehead, smiling into her incredulous eyes. 'Now that I know the truth, it seems all too obvious. You're so much like her, not so much in looks as in character . . .'

But Giulia was hardly listening to him. 'The Prioress . . . is my mother!' She was filled with an overwhelming sense of joy and relief. So many memories came crowding into her mind—Mother Maria's cool, detached manner when first they met, that must have concealed such a poignant conflict of emotions; her strength, her kindness, her quiet air of authority. How wise she had been not to marry Ercole Tebaldi! They would have made a disastrously ill-matched couple . . . and yet they had remained friends long after all passion between them had died.

And Monna Lucia, who had been so obsequious today in the presence of the Prioress—how astounded *she* would be if she knew the truth!

'I'm a Martinelli,' Giulia murmured, half to herself. 'And the Procurator is my uncle! My mother must have told him so in that letter she wrote to him—and that's why he agreed to help me . . .' She sat up so abruptly that the gondola rocked beneath them. 'I must go to her!'

'No.' Pietro drew her back against him. 'She said that, once you knew, it was best you shouldn't meet again. Her part in your life is over, though she thanked God she was given the chance to help you to find happiness. But now your happiness is my concern.' He bent to kiss her lips. 'And I gave her my solemn word that I shall cherish you always, to the end of my days.' He kissed her again, with increasing passion, and after only a moment's hesitation Giulia surrendered, knowing that the Prioress had spoken with her customary wisdom.

Without taking his mouth from hers, Pietro pulled the curtains of the cabin, enclosing them in a small secret world of their own. Soon they were oblivious to everything but each other as the gondola bore them homeward, while outside all Venice was noisily celebrating the approach of summer and the promise of another year's fruitful union with the sea.

Masquerade Historical Romances

From the golden days of romance

The days of real romance are vividly recreated in Masquerade Historical Romances, published by Mills & Boon. Secret assignations, high intrigues – all are portrayed against authentic historical backgrounds. This is the other Masquerade title to look out for this month.

LADY OF FLAME
by Ann Edgeworth

From a comfortable house in Victorian London to a dilapidated cocoa plantation in the West Indies, flame-haired Triona Brooks follows her disgraced husband with naive trust. But under the tropical sun of Ste-Martine she is forced at last to recognise his irresponsibility when he abandons her. Left alone on the estate, Triona turns to their ruthless and mysterious neighbour, Duncan Ross for help. And *he* responds first by offering advice — and then love…

Mills & Boon
the rose of romance

Masquerade Historical Romances

New romances from bygone days

Masquerade Historical Romances, published by Mills & Boon, vividly recreate the romance of our past. These are the two superb new stories to look out for next month.

RACHEL AND THE VISCOUNT
Alanna Wilson

THE POLISH WOLF
Janet Edmonds

Buy them from your usual paperback stockist, or write to: Mills & Boon Reader Service, P.O. Box 236, Thornton Rd, Croydon, Surrey CR9 3RU, England. Readers in South Africa - write to: Mills & Boon Reader Service of Southern Africa, Private Bag X3010, Randburg, 2125.

**Mills & Boon
the rose of romance**